BILLY GOAT TALES

THE BRIDGE TO
BITCOIN

RICH SMOTHERS

COPYRIGHT © 2024
ALL RIGHTS RESERVED

DISCLAIMER

A Children's Folk Tale inspires this tale, 'The Three Billy Goats Gruff,' retold by Mac Barnett.

DEDICATION

This book is dedicated to the Billy Goat Tales Team—Tony Baeza, Jeff Dingess, Christian Lugaro and Jimmy Wyble.

ACKNOWLEDGMENT

Martin Hansell holds a special place in my heart for inspiring this book. Billy Goat Tales is a community of like-minded people working to serve the Cryptocurrency Community. We believe in a "Givers Gain" philosophy and work to provide guidance and support to our members. Martin was able to see the parallel between the Three Billy Goats Gruff folk tale and the service we provide to our community, which inspired me to write this book.

PROLOGUE

In the realm of digital innovation, a bridge emerges, connecting ordinary lives to the allure of Bitcoin. Yet, beneath its promise lies a lurking danger—a troll named Scammer-Delete, preying on unsuspecting travelers. As seekers flock to the Bridge to Bitcoin, hope collides with deception. But amidst the chaos emerges a champion: Billy Goat, protector of the vulnerable. He illuminates the path to safety with each step, thwarting the troll's sinister schemes. This is a tale of courage, resilience, and the enduring power of community in the face of adversity—a journey through the Blockchain realm and across the Bridge to Bitcoin, where triumph awaits the bold.

Once upon a time, there was a blockchain bridge to new opportunities and great wealth.

The opportunity was so wonderfully appealing that more and more people wanted it.

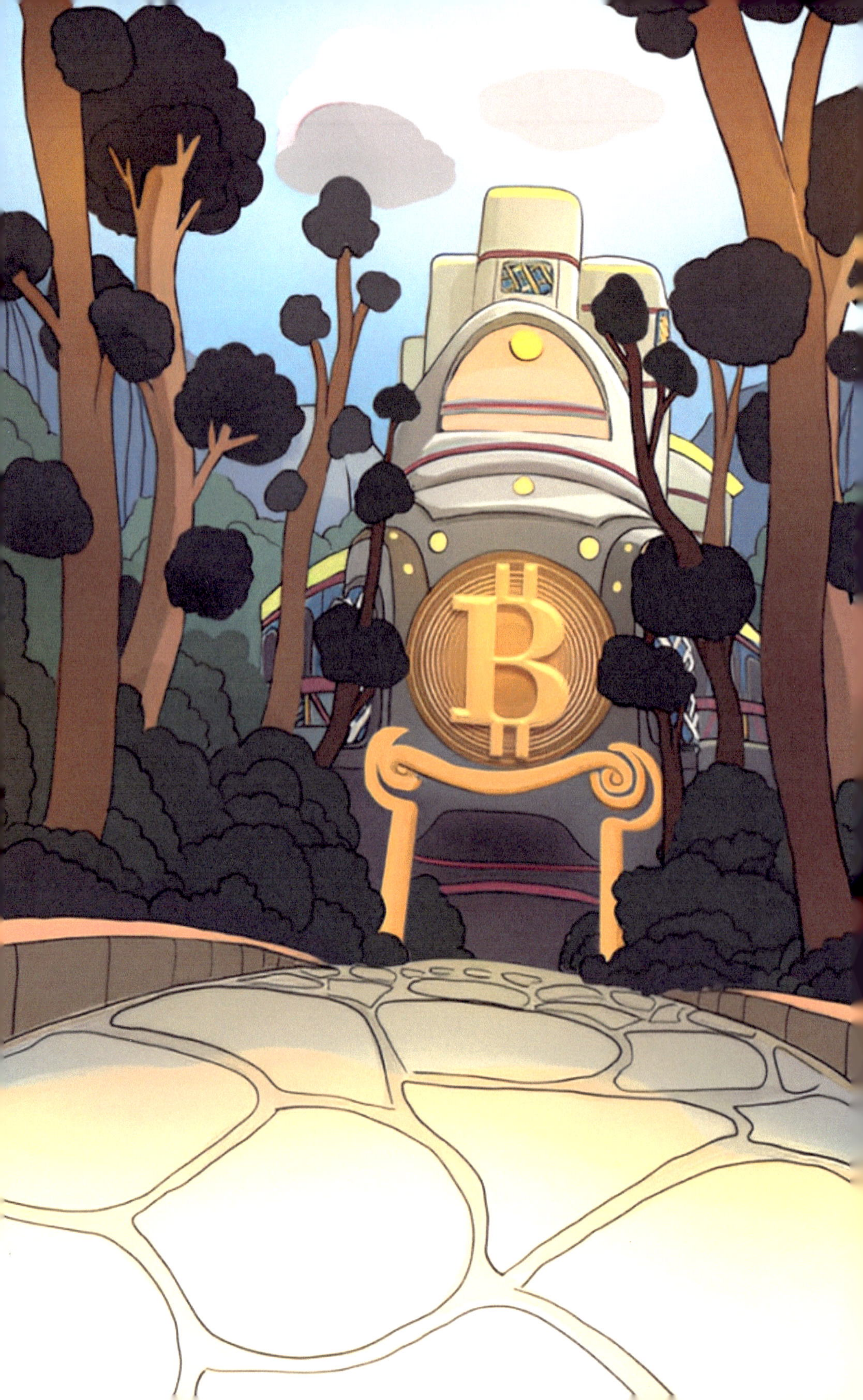

However, users had to cross the Blockchain Bridge to obtain the opportunity.

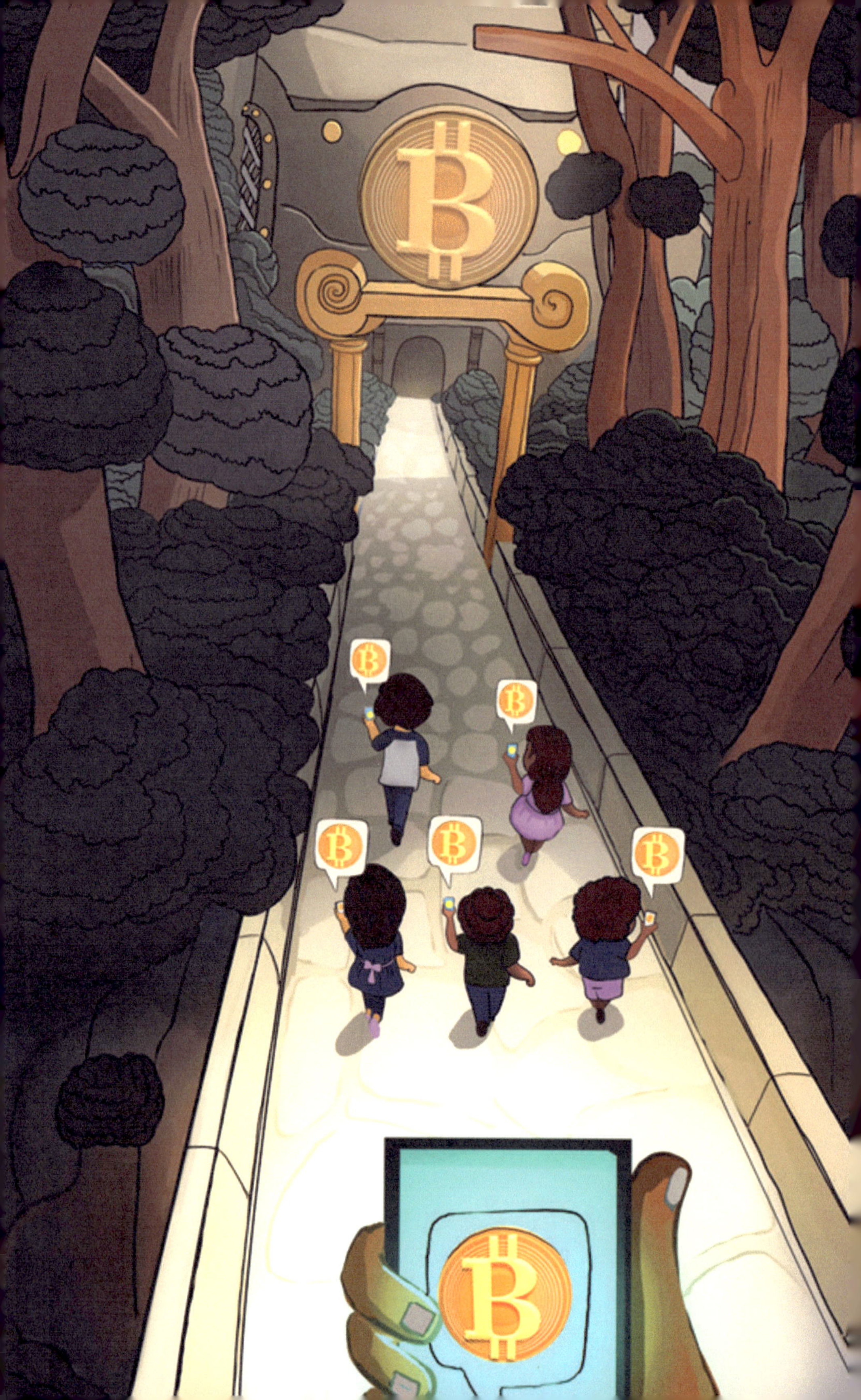

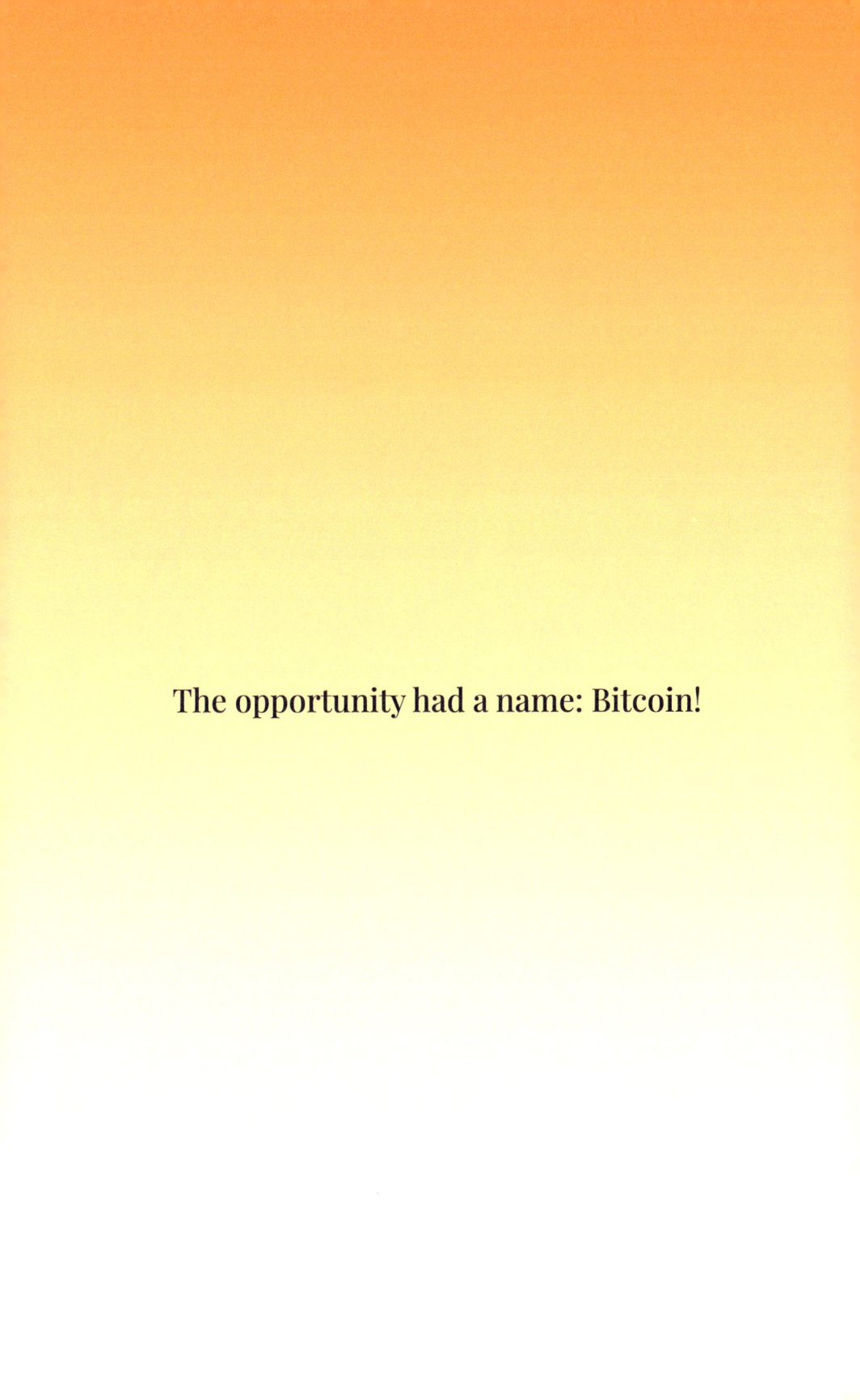

The opportunity had a name: Bitcoin!

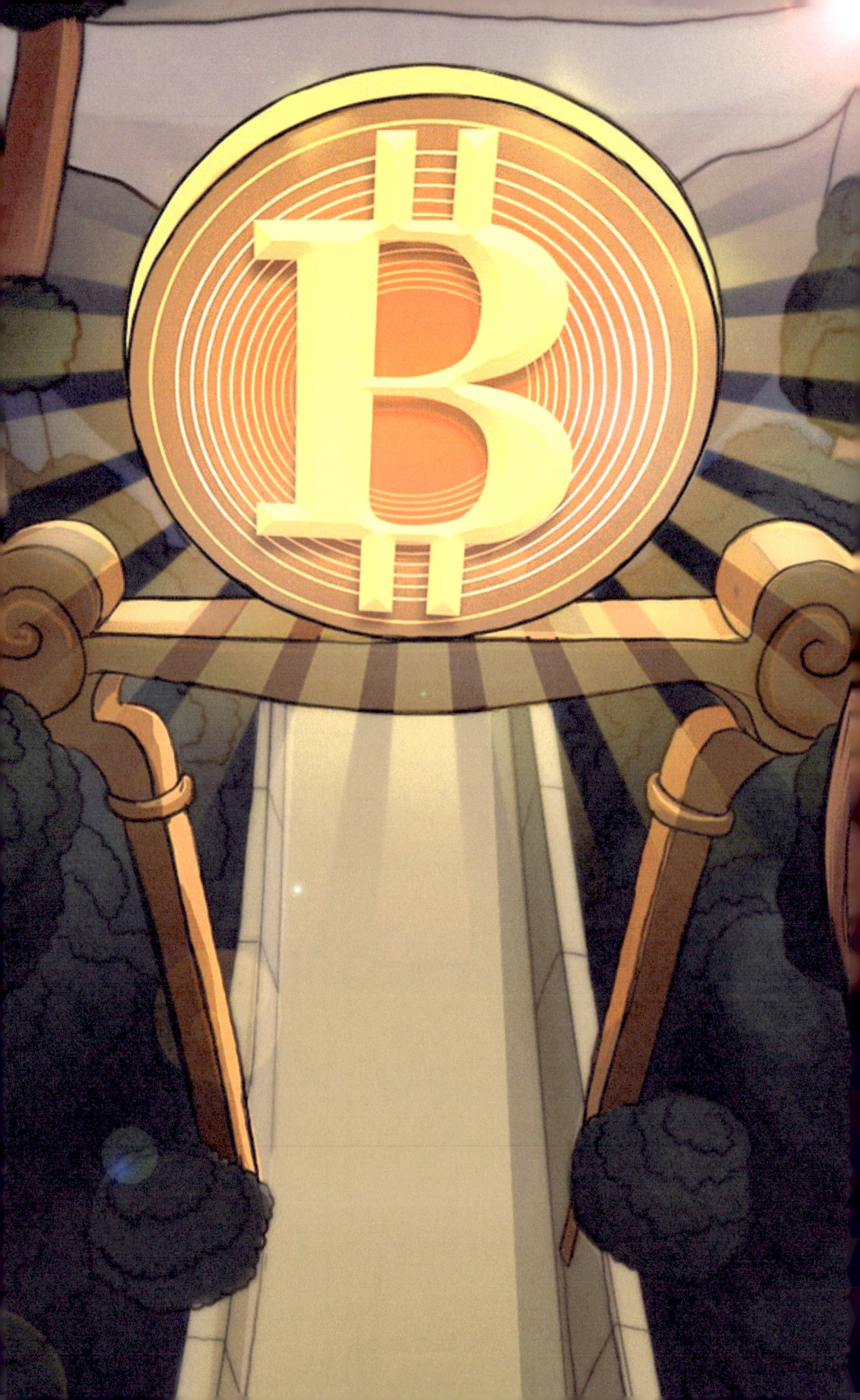

Beneath the bridge, there lived a **hungry Troll.**

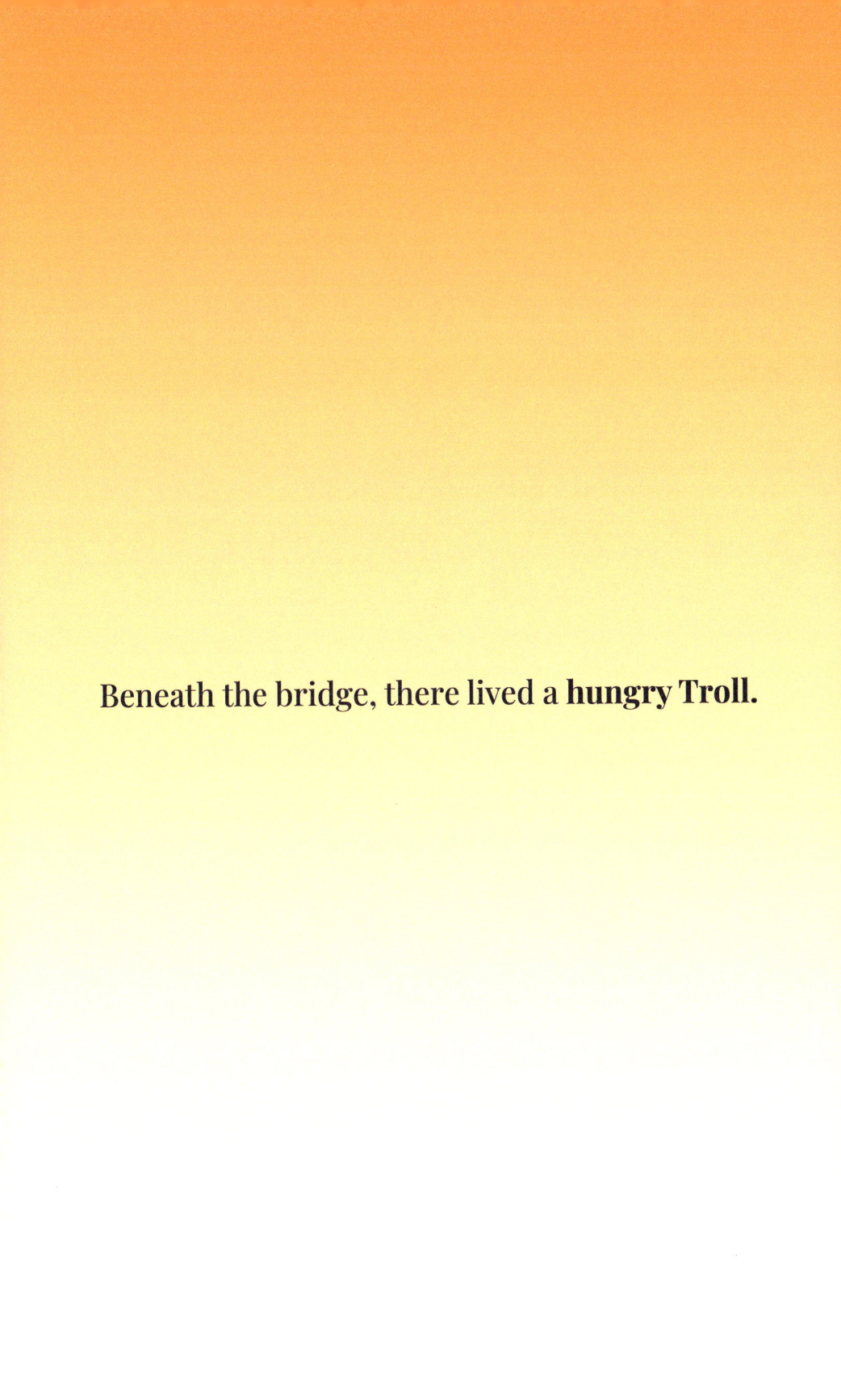

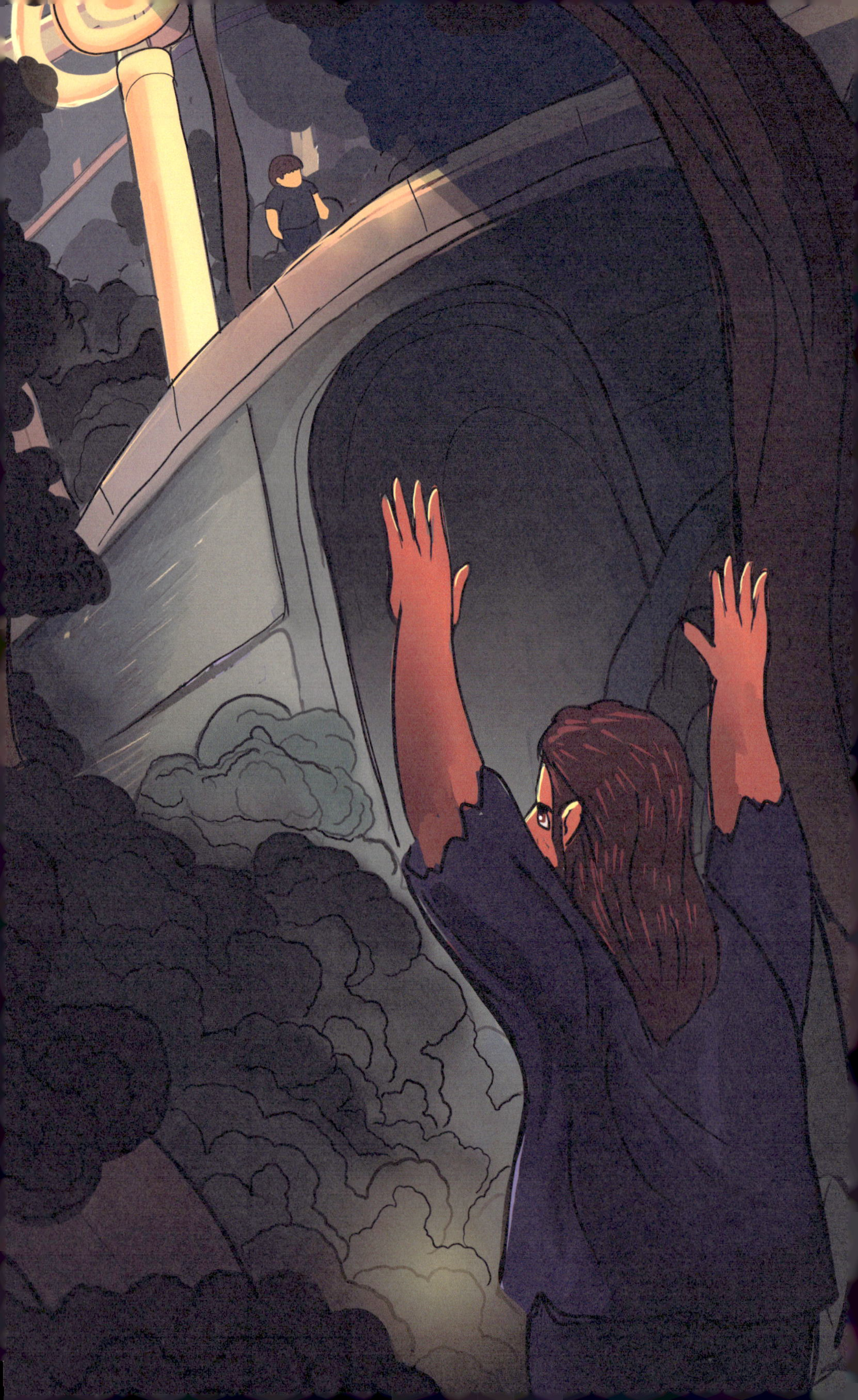

The Troll would sit under the bridge listening and waiting, hoping for someone to cross the bridge above his head. Hoping to snag a new user entering the Blockchain Bridge to Bitcoin.

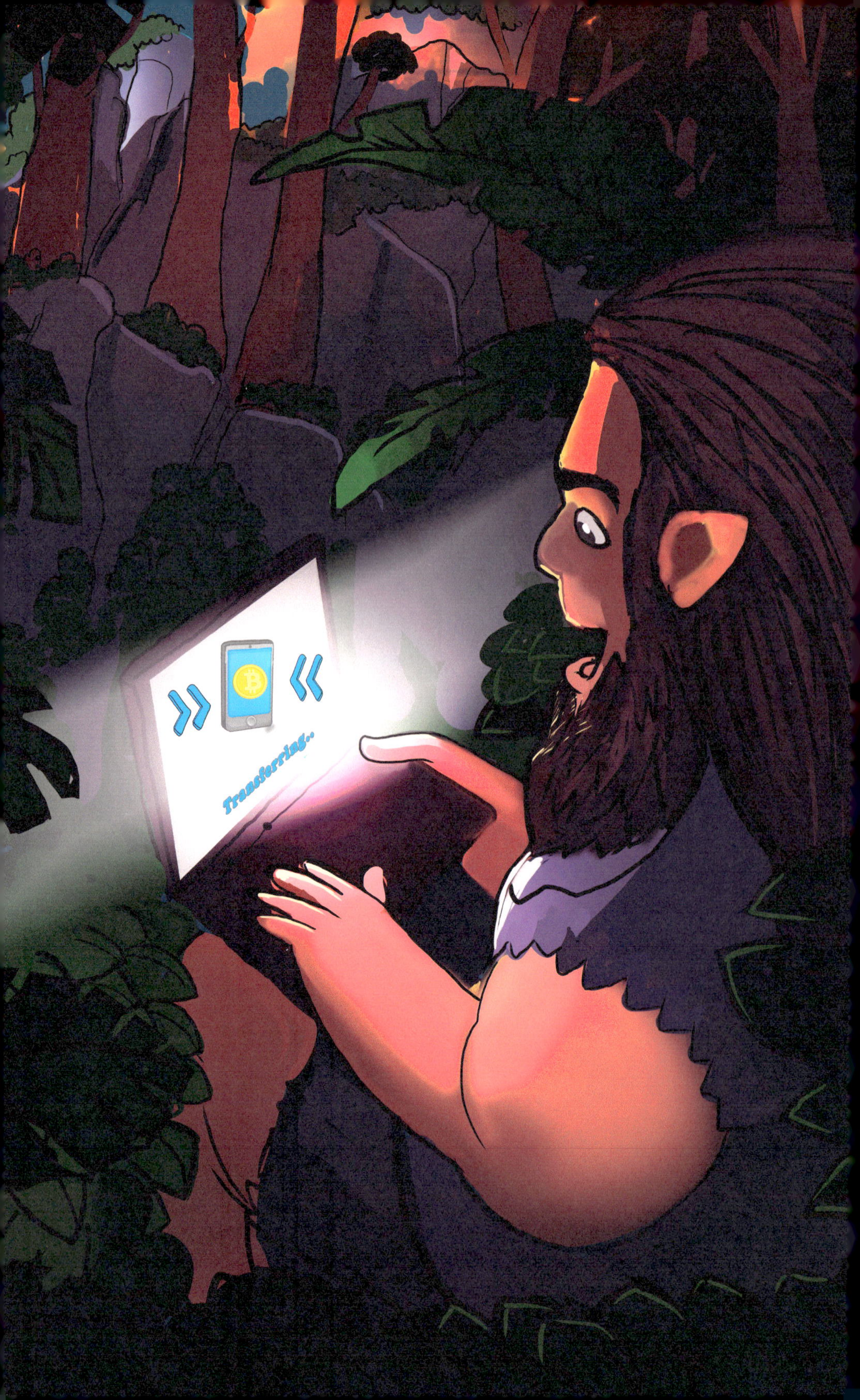
Transferring..

"I am a troll, I love to eat, and the digital footprint left in a Tweet. I create fake posts, websites and wallets to attract my prey like a bolt to a socket. I work daily, spinning webs like a spider, hoping to catch you as your trust grows wider."

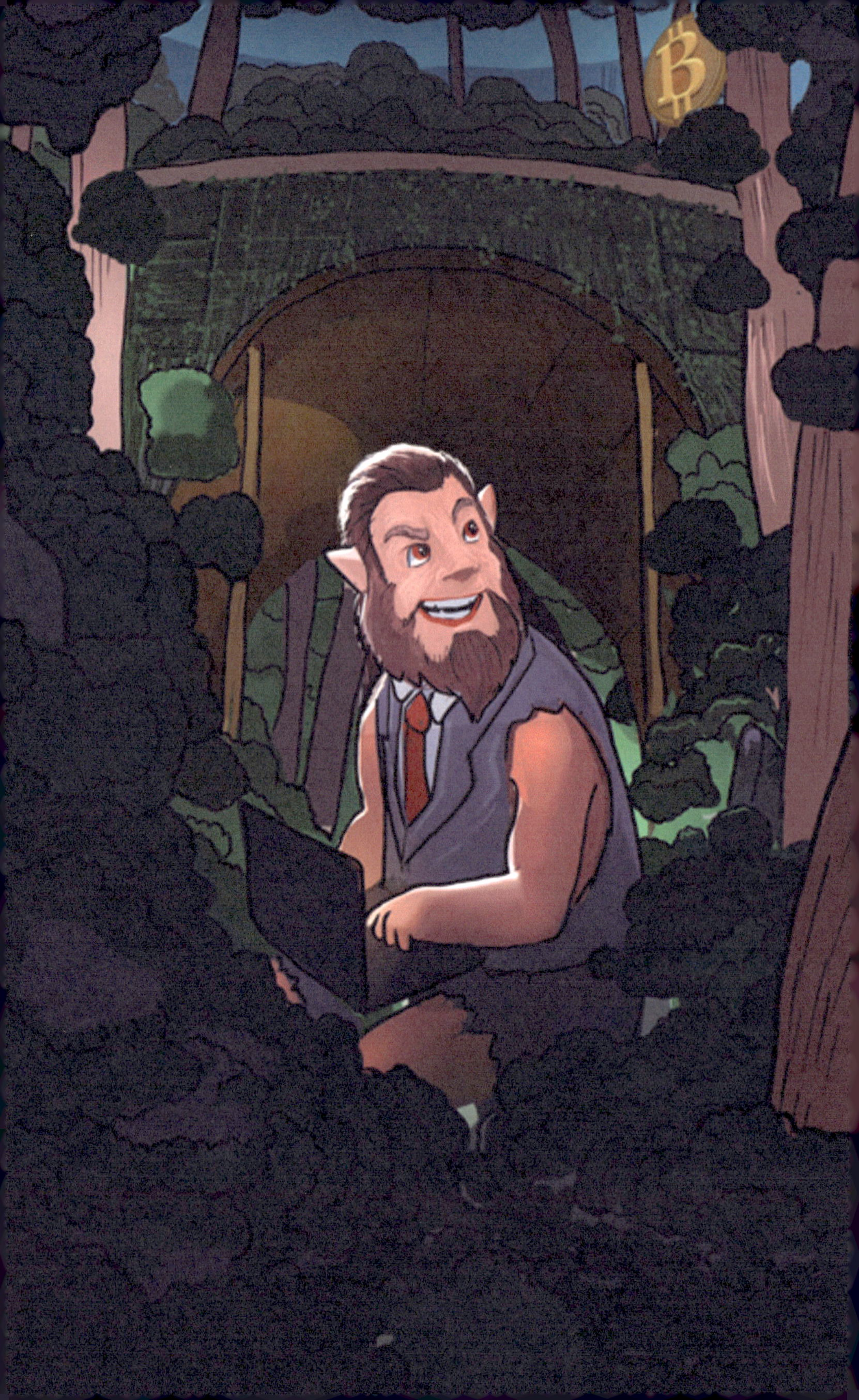

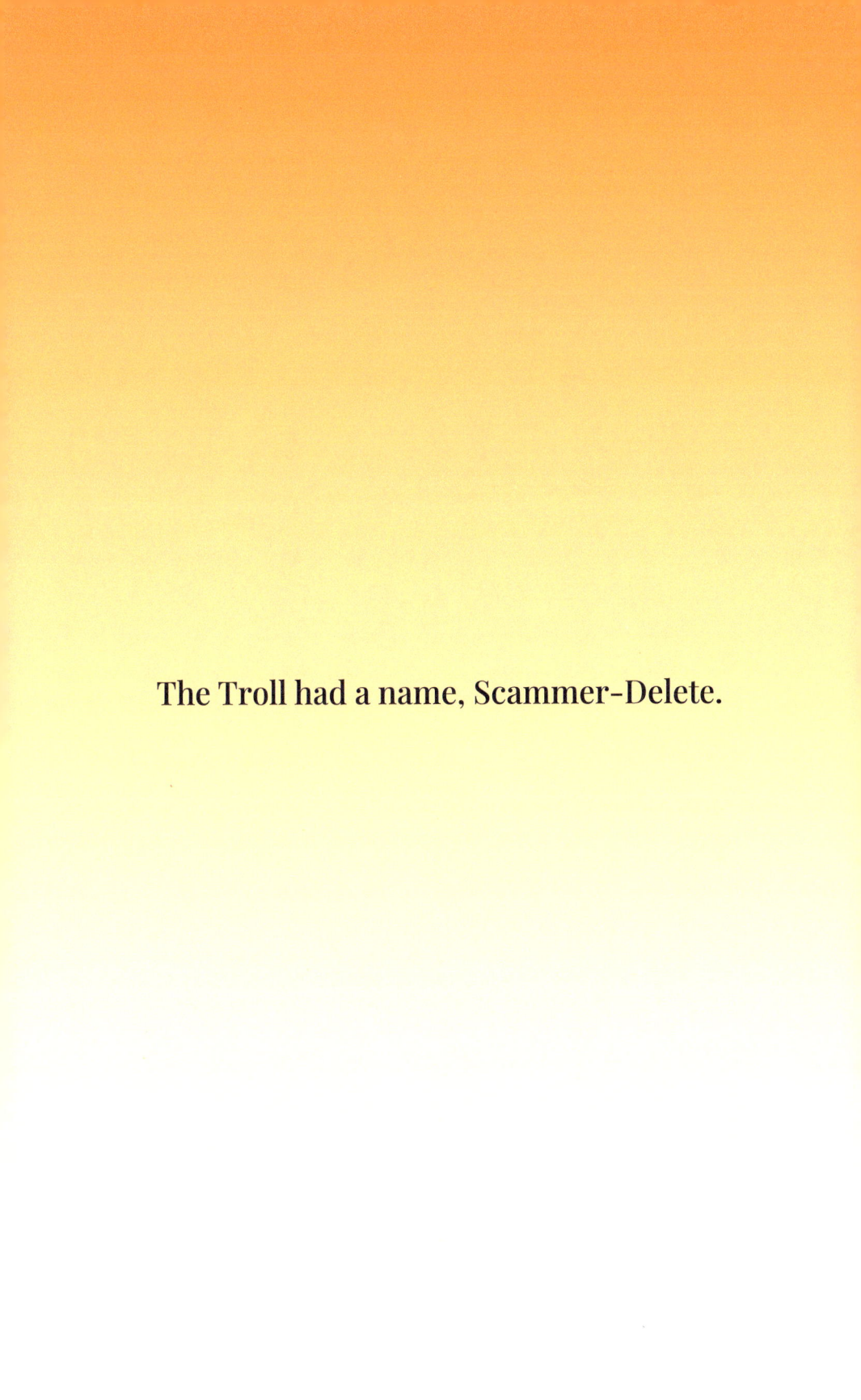

The Troll had a name, Scammer-Delete.

SCAMMER-DELETE

As the opportunity grew, with only one way in, the bridge seemed narrow like goats in a pen. "Ding, dong! Ding, dong!" went the bridge above his head, an email alert; he was about to be fed!

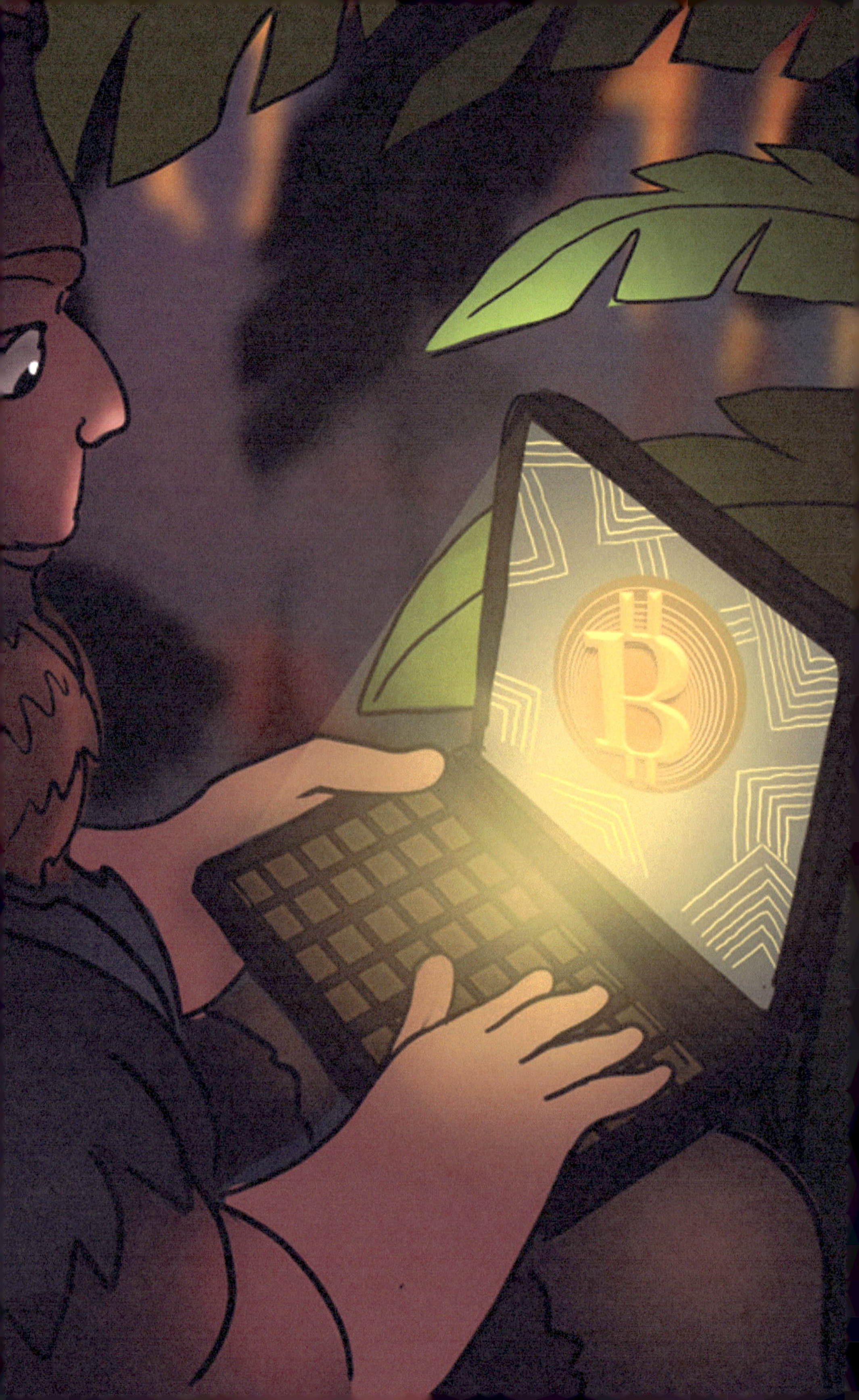

"Who seeks to reach Bitcoin, who wants to build wealth, my bridge is safe, come and find out".

"My first name is Gruffy, and my last name is Goat. I want to make riches; that is my hope."

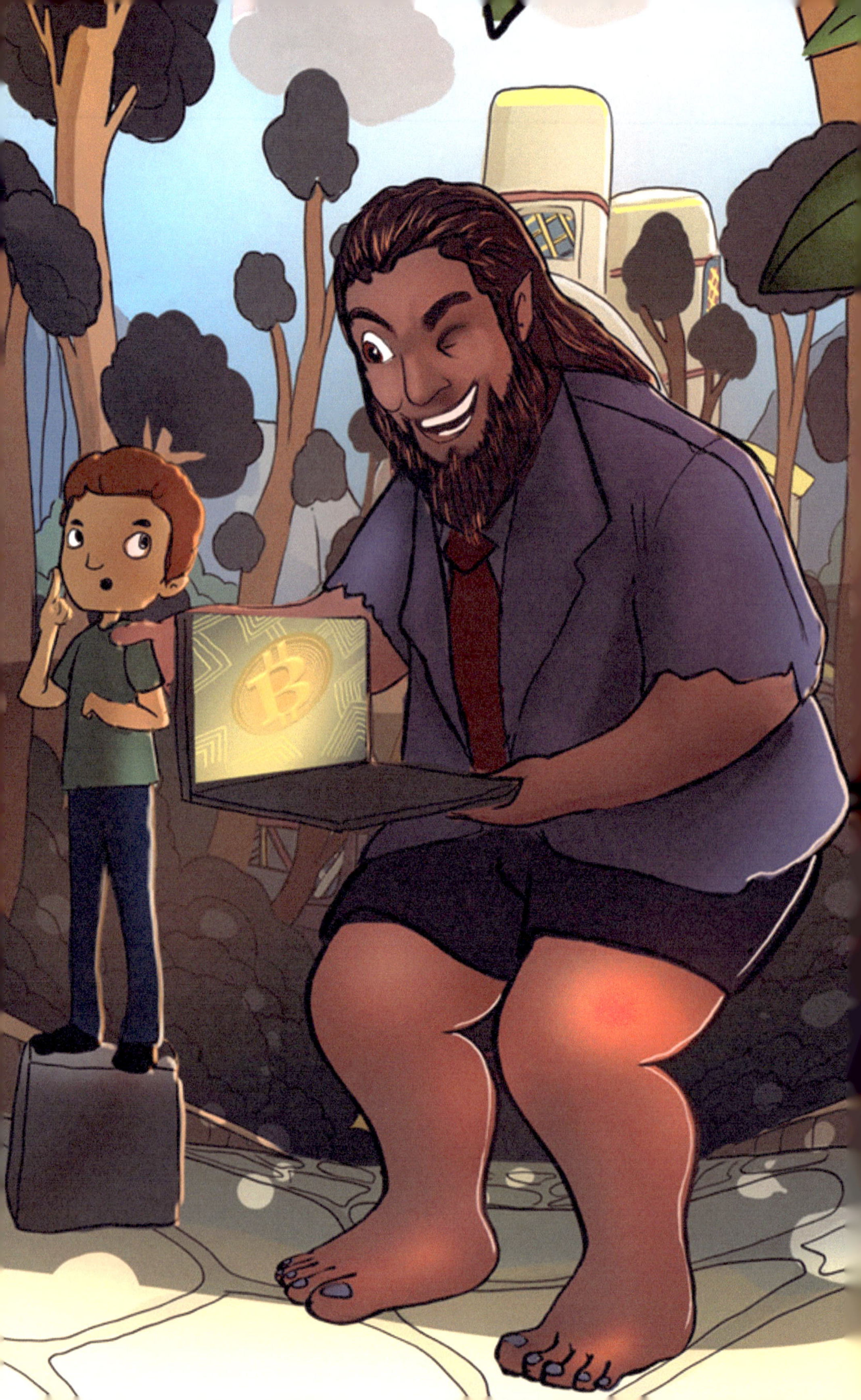

A new subscriber had just created a wallet, oblivious to the danger he would encounter.

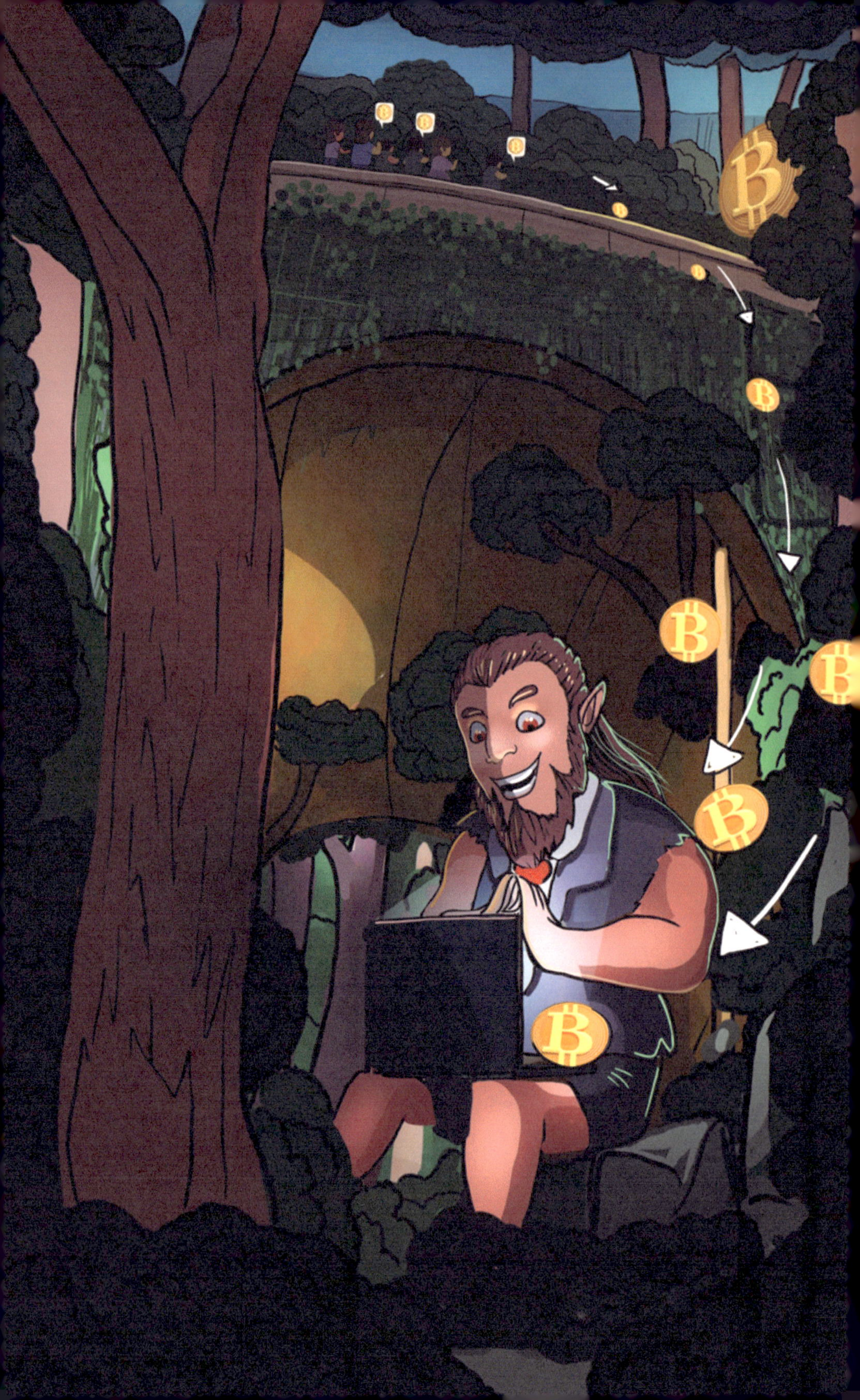

"Come a bit closer and click on my link; I shall fill up your wallet", the troll said with a wink.

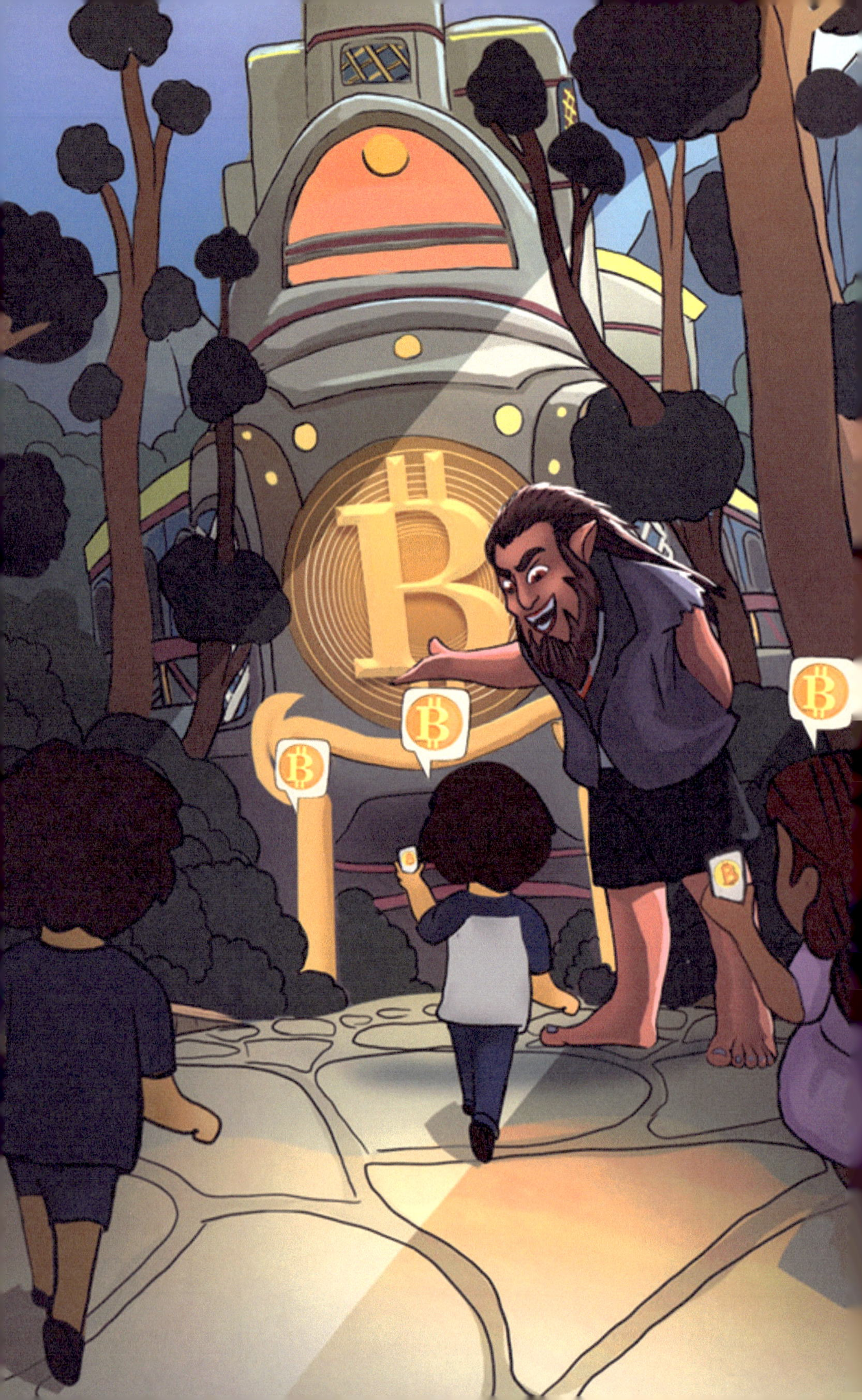

"My brother Billy has warned me about you, Mr. Delete; if you let me pass, Billy will click on your link. He has lots of money and NFTs the size of a whale, wait and see!"

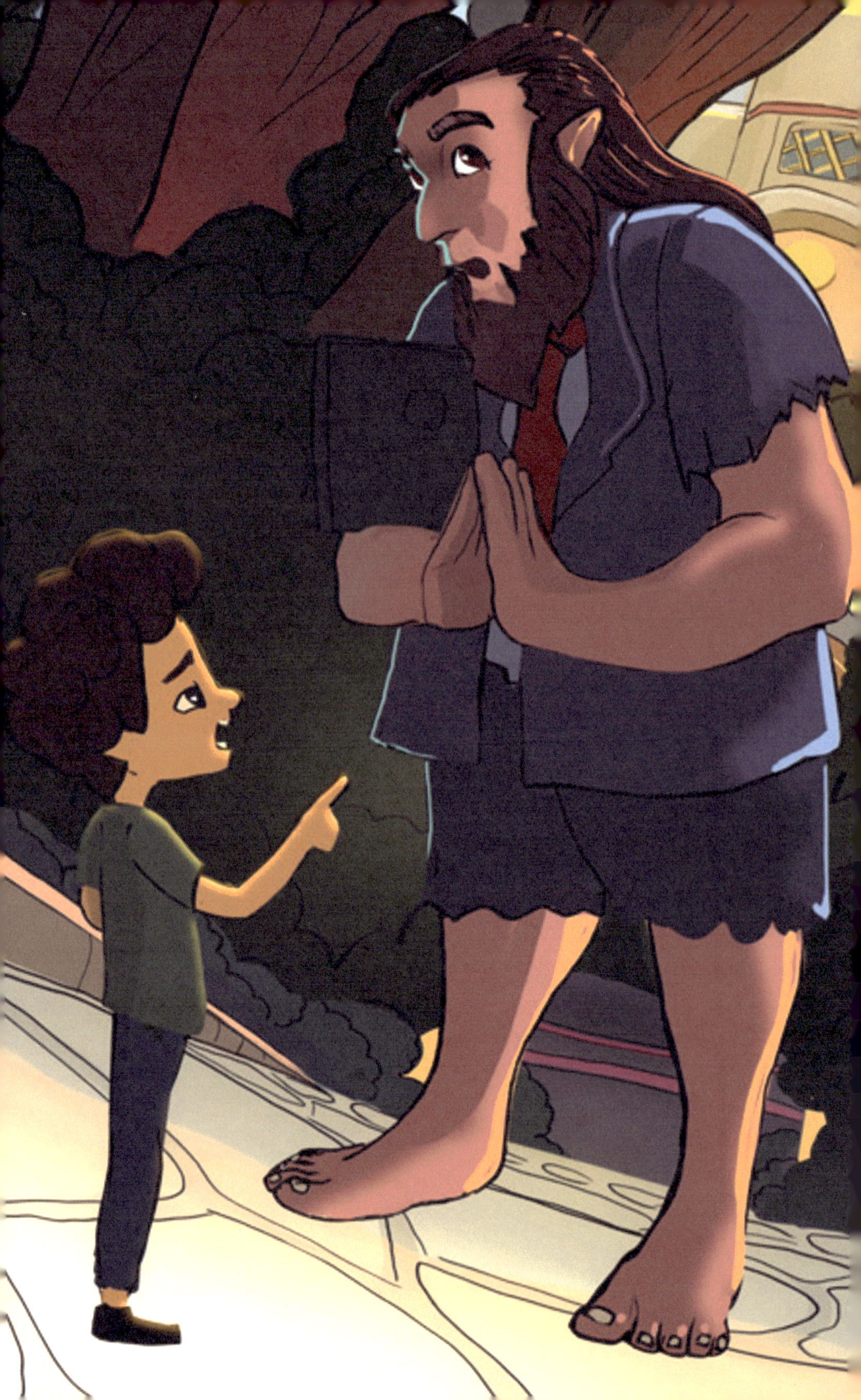

The troll was hungry and needed to eat, but kept thinking about Billy, a mouth-watering treat.

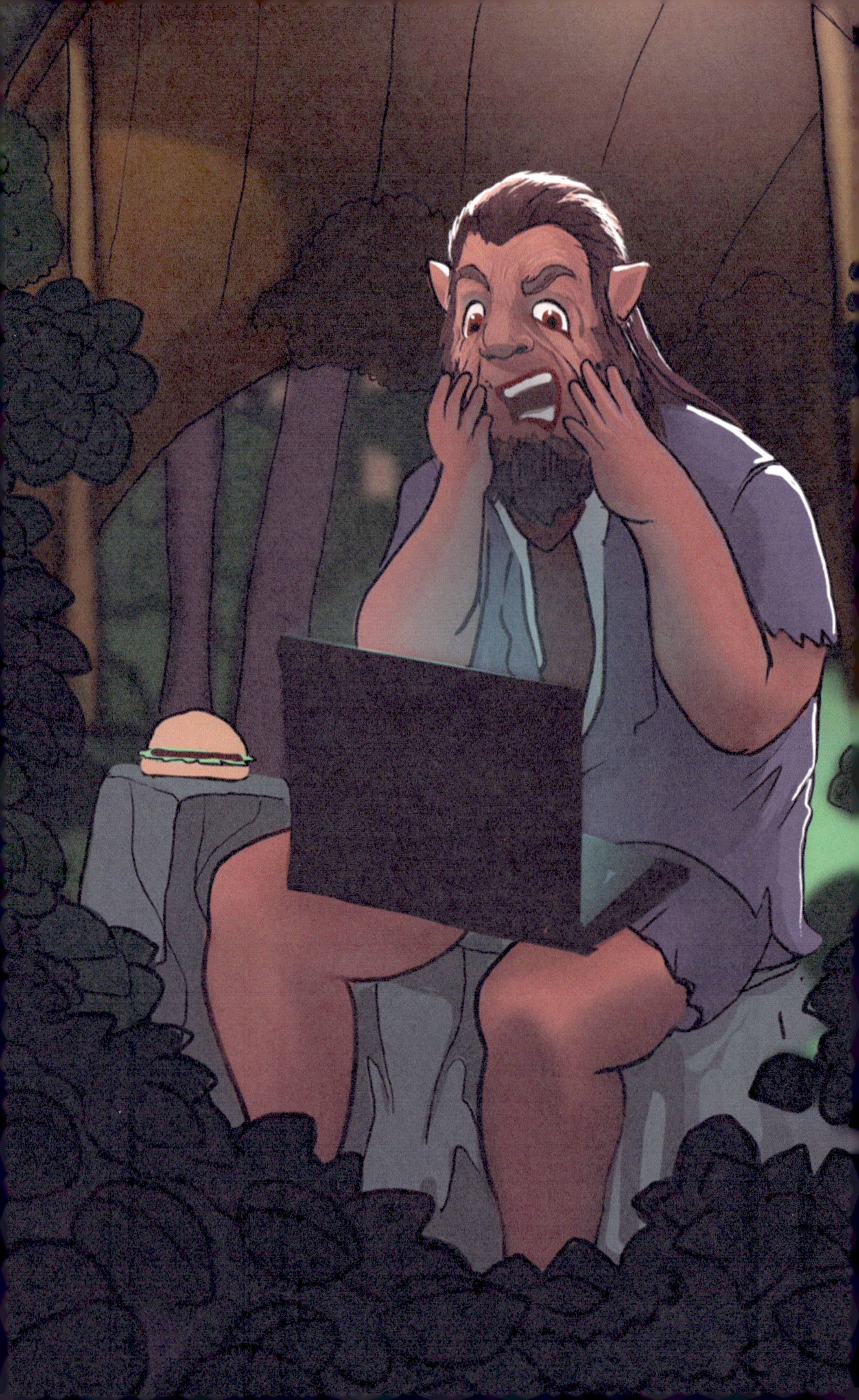

The Troll was frustrated but yelled, "Consider yourself lucky you did not click on my link; I will be waiting for Billy, a much bigger treat."

The troll was content, knowing another would arrive; the bridge to Bitcoin was coming alive.

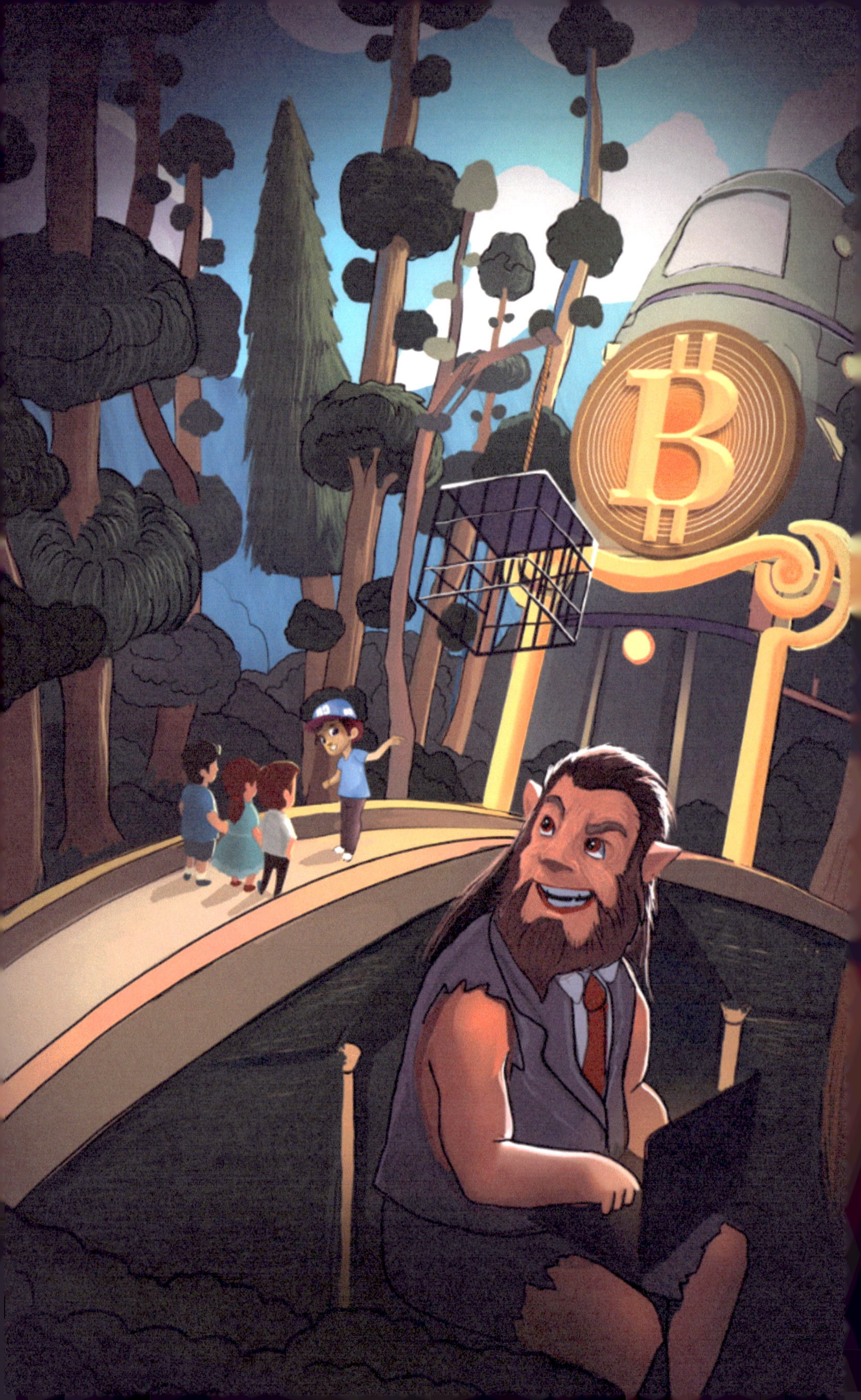

The troll kept creating many more apps; he was growing wealthy from all his traps.

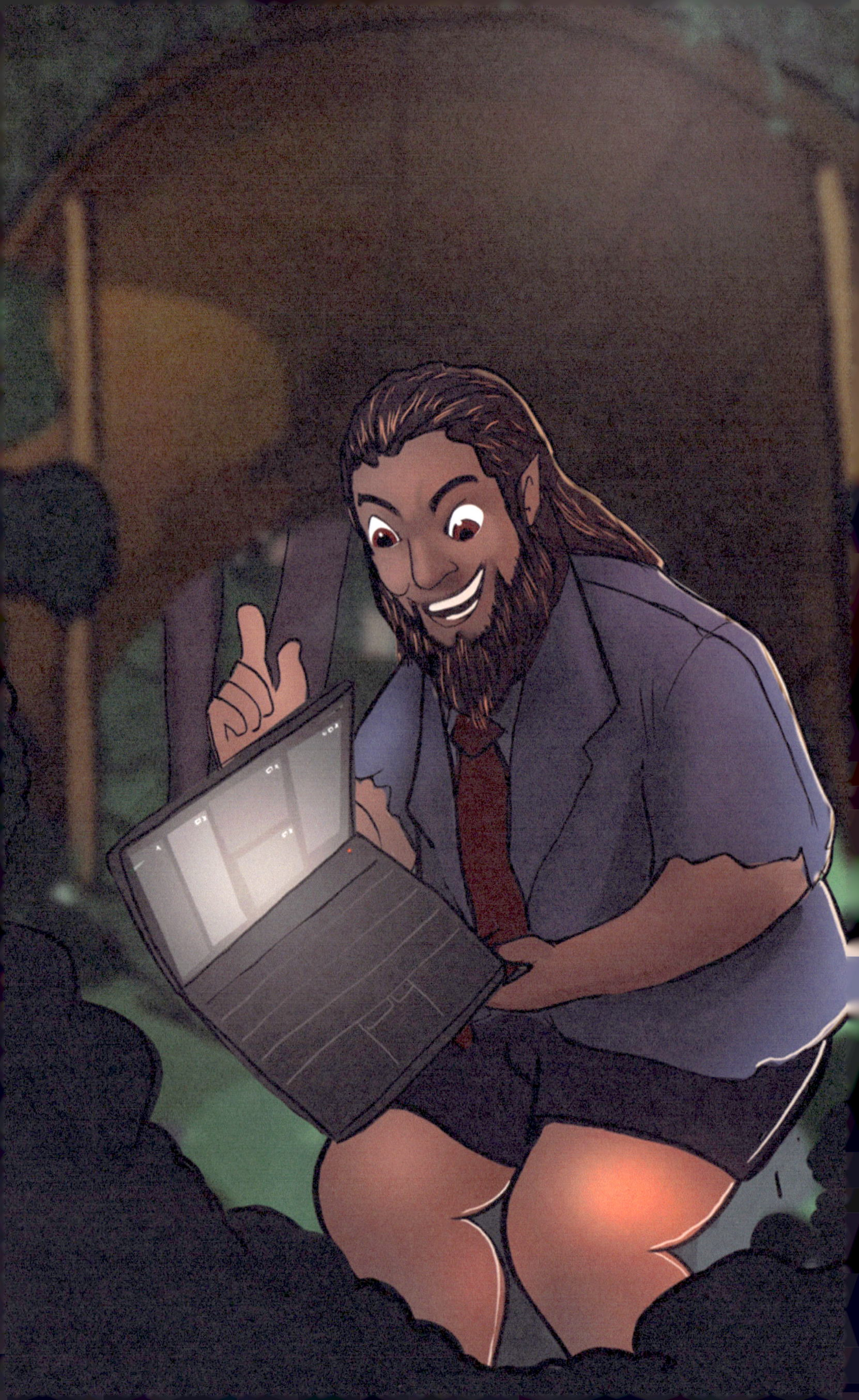

"Ding, dong! Ding, dong," went the bridge above his head, the sweet sound of an email; he knew he would be fed! "Who seeks to reach Bitcoin, who wants to build wealth, my bridge is safe? Come and find out."

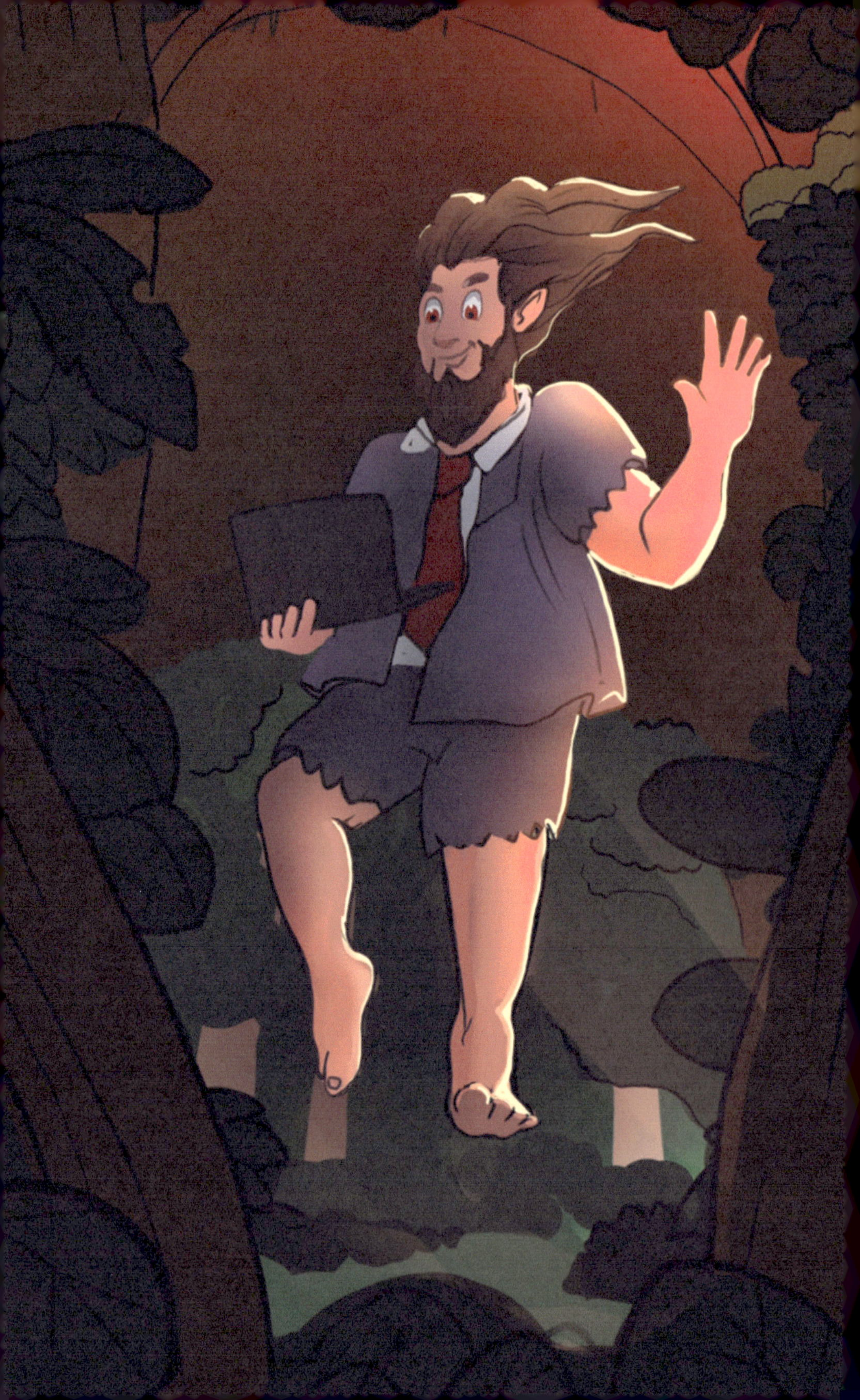

"My first name is Jimmy, and my last name is Goat. I want to make riches; that is my hope. Jimmy was new to crypto and had just created a wallet, oblivious to the danger he would encounter.

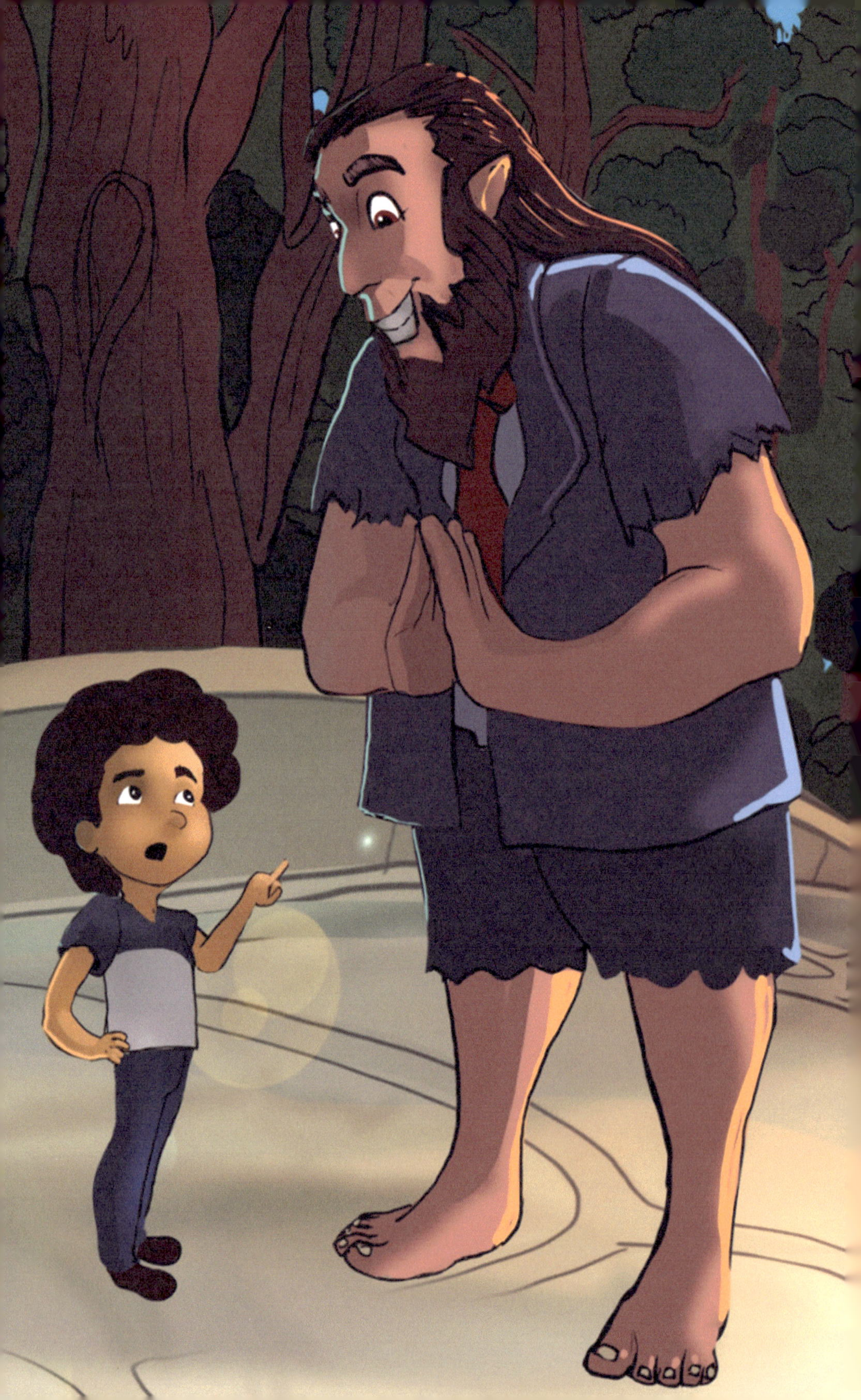

The troll answered, "Come a bit closer and click on my link; I shall fill up your wallet," the troll said with a wink.

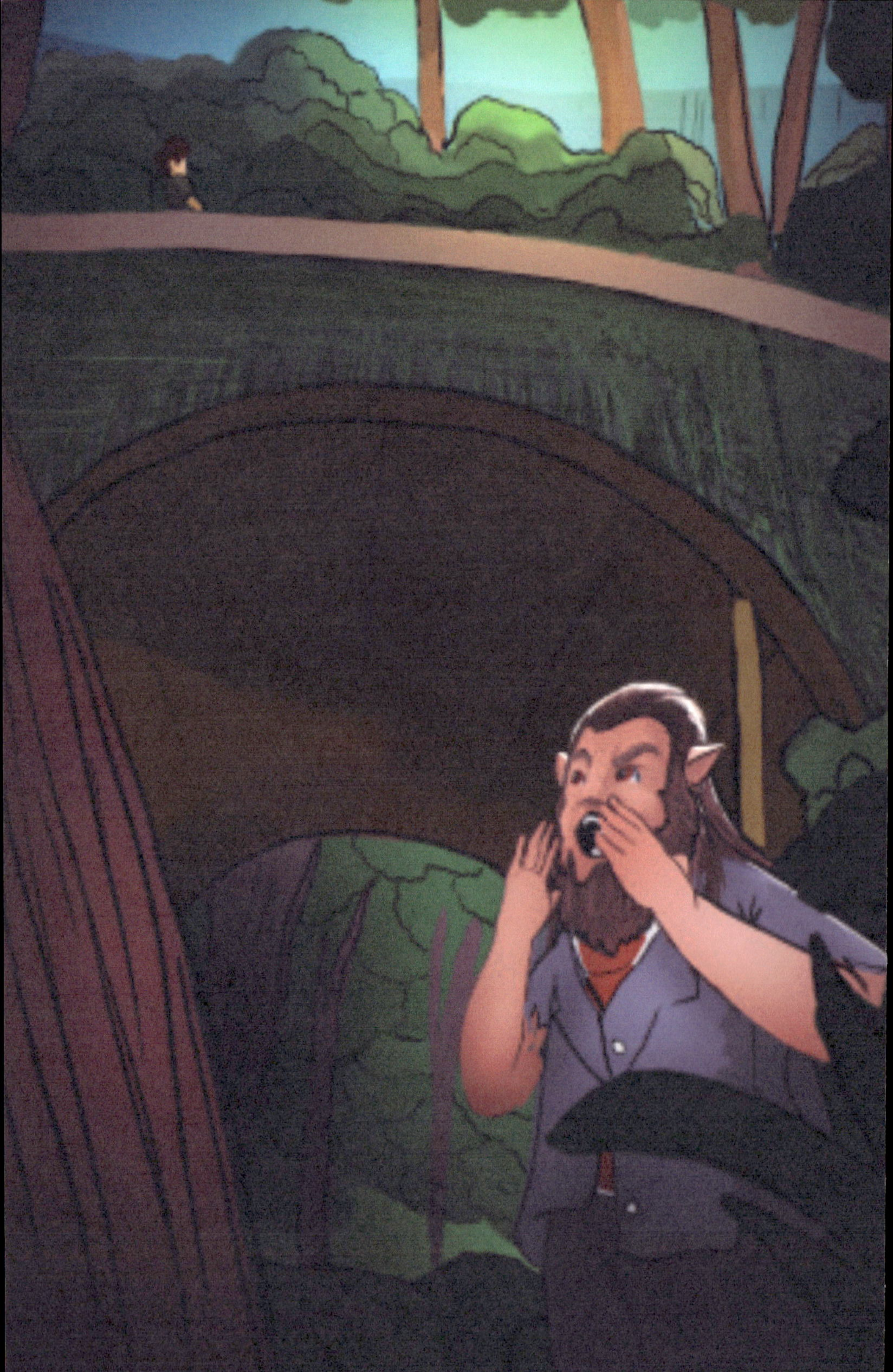

"My brother Billy has warned me about you, Mr. Delete; if you let me pass, Billy will click on your link. He has lots of money and NFTs the size of a whale, wait and see!"

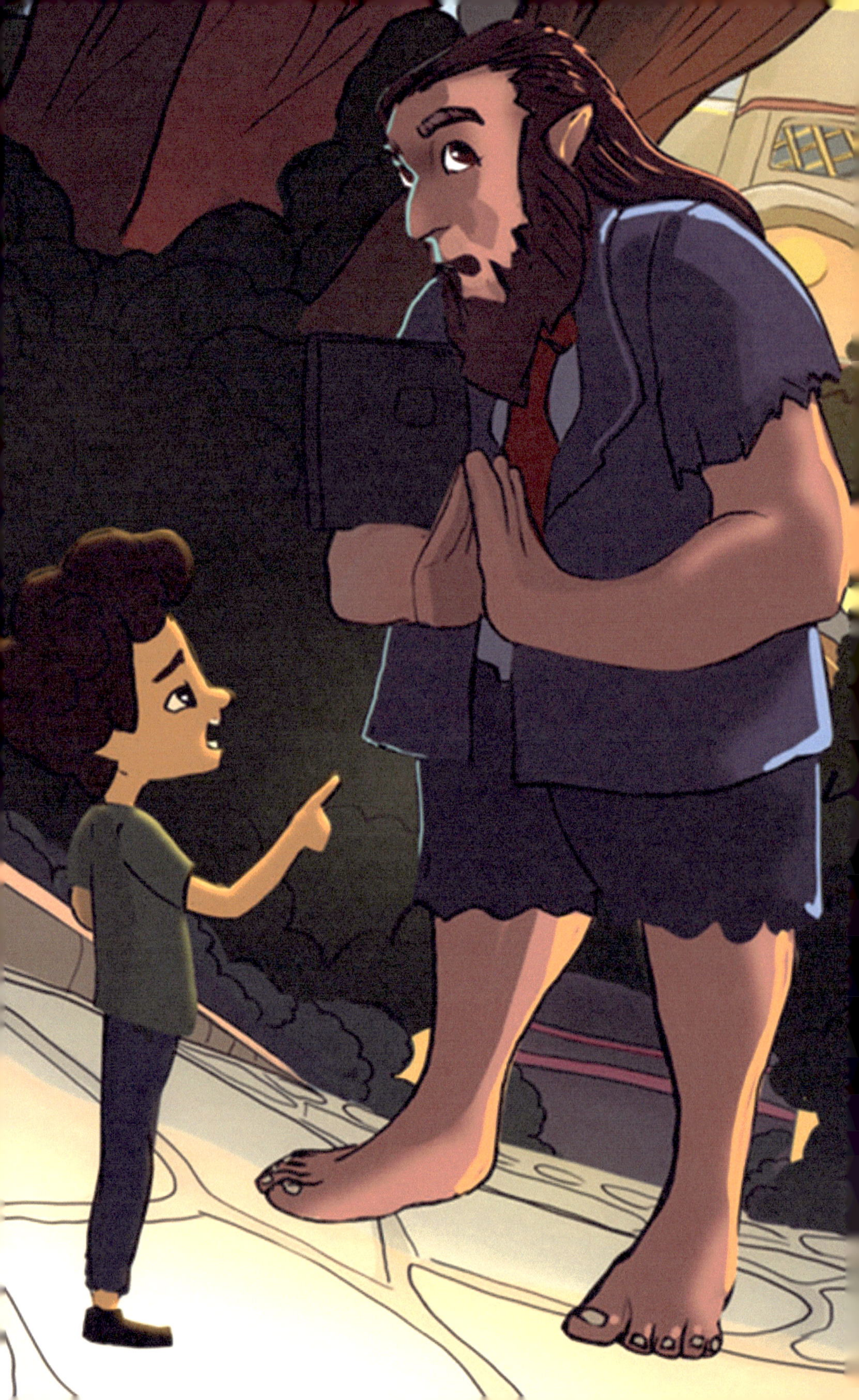

The troll was hungry and needed to eat but kept thinking about Billy, a mouth-watering treat.

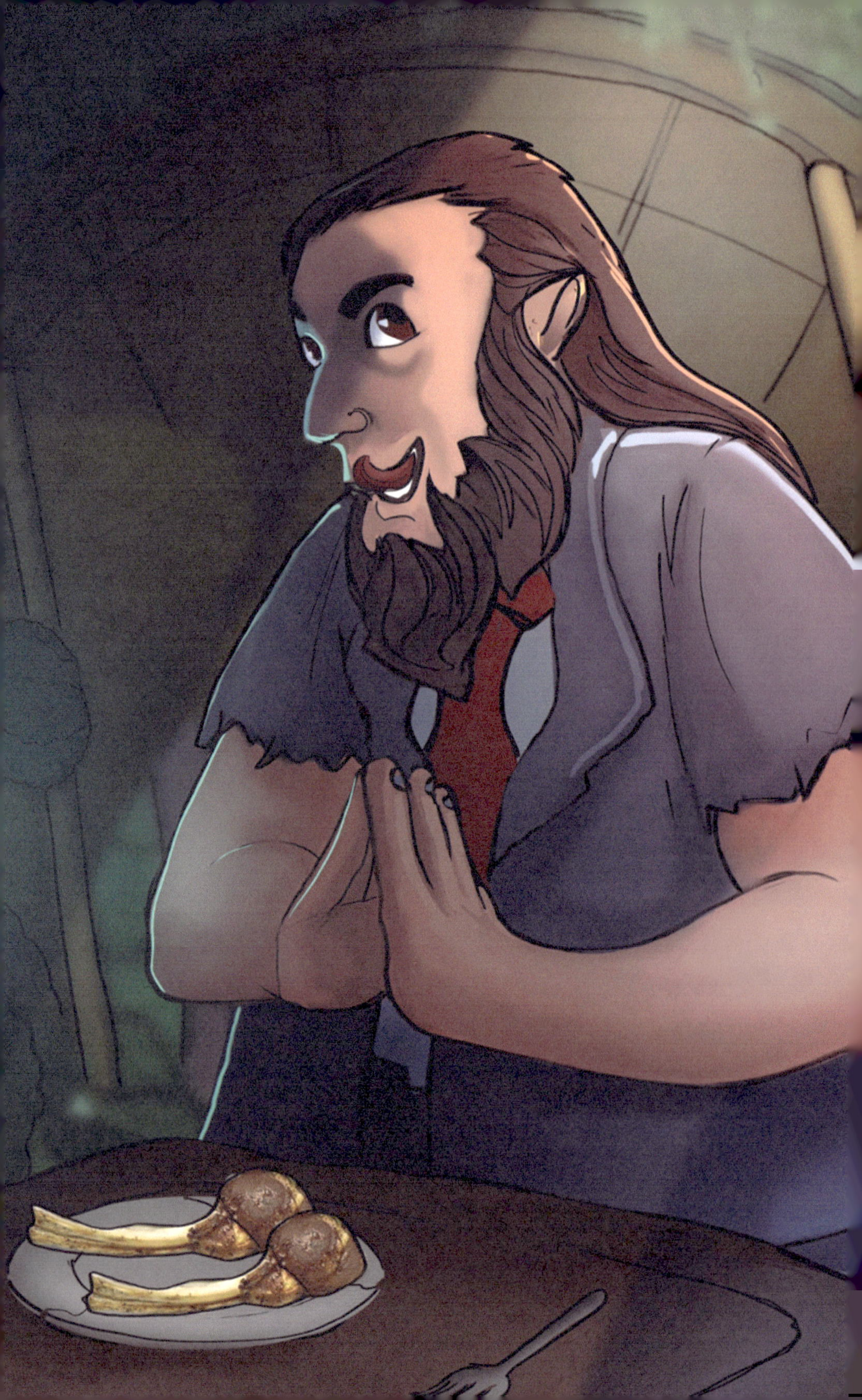

The troll yelled, "Consider yourself lucky you did not click on my link; I will be waiting for Billy, a much bigger treat.

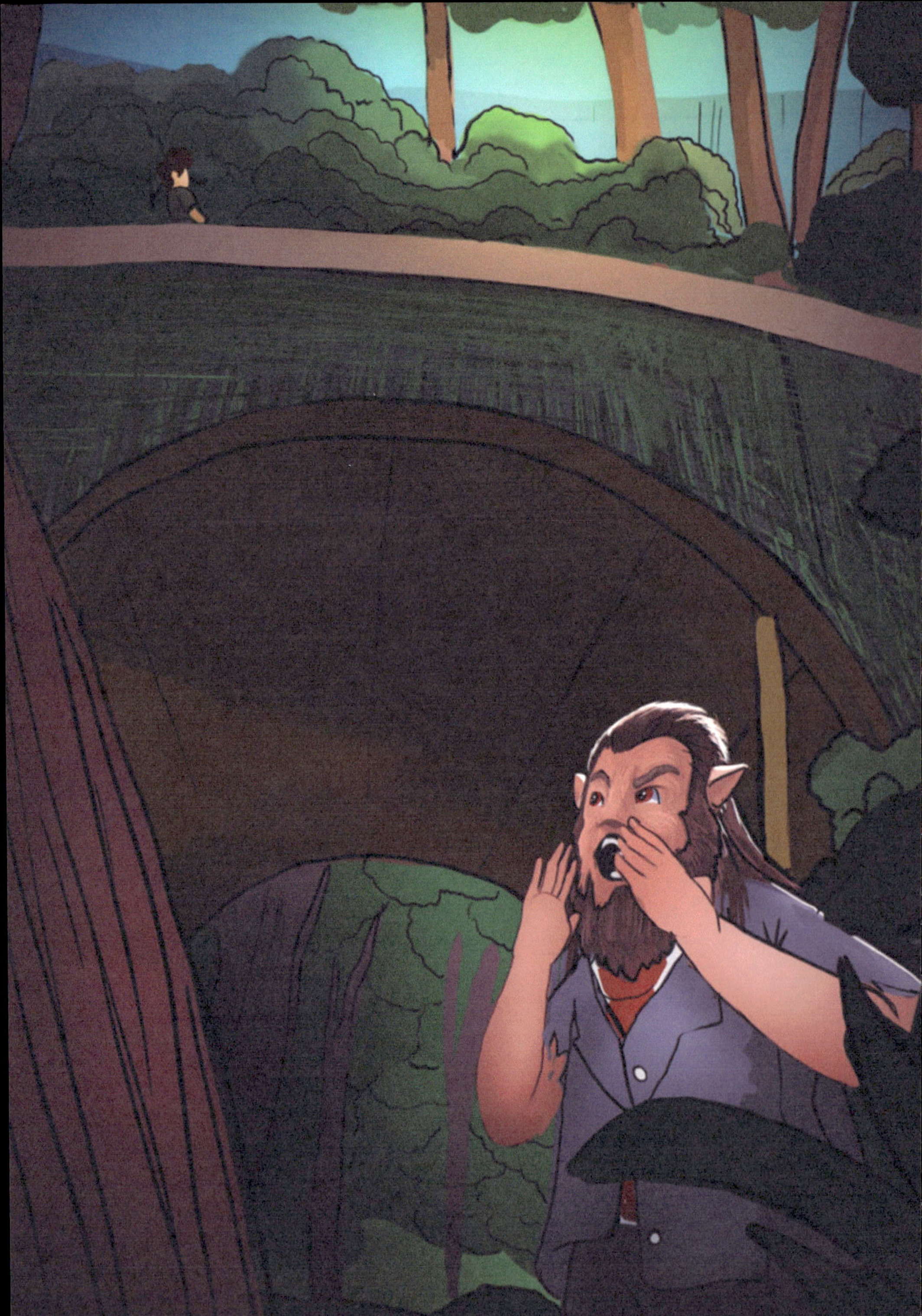

The troll kept building, creating more fake posts, websites and wallets. Each day, he snagged many users trying to cross the blockchain bridge to Bitcoin. But day after day, he waited for Billy, a whale-of-a-treat.

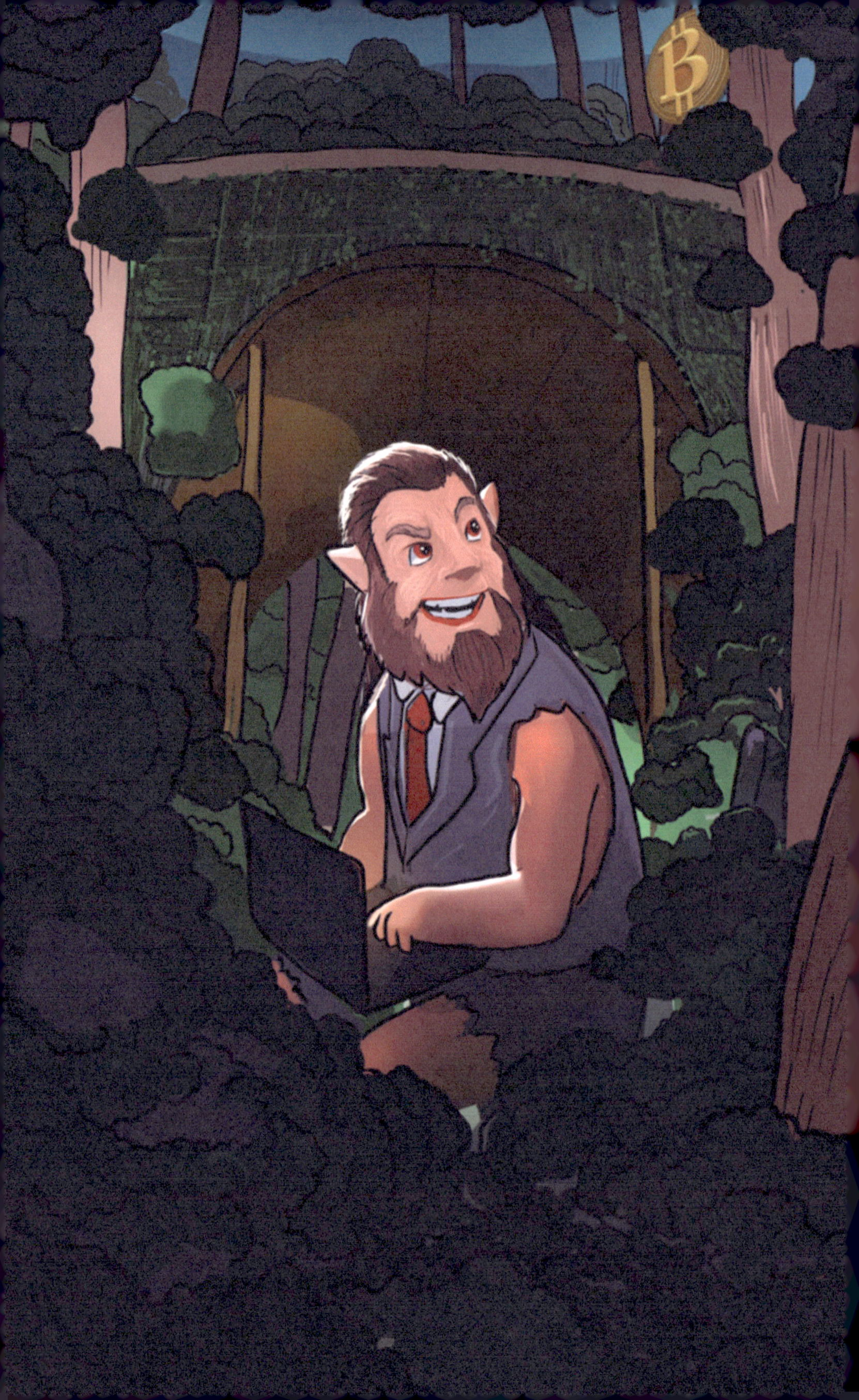

"Ding, dong! Ding dong," went the bridge above his head, another alert; he hoped to be fed. "Who seeks to reach Bitcoin? the Troll happily asked. "Who dares to run across my bridge, moving so fast?

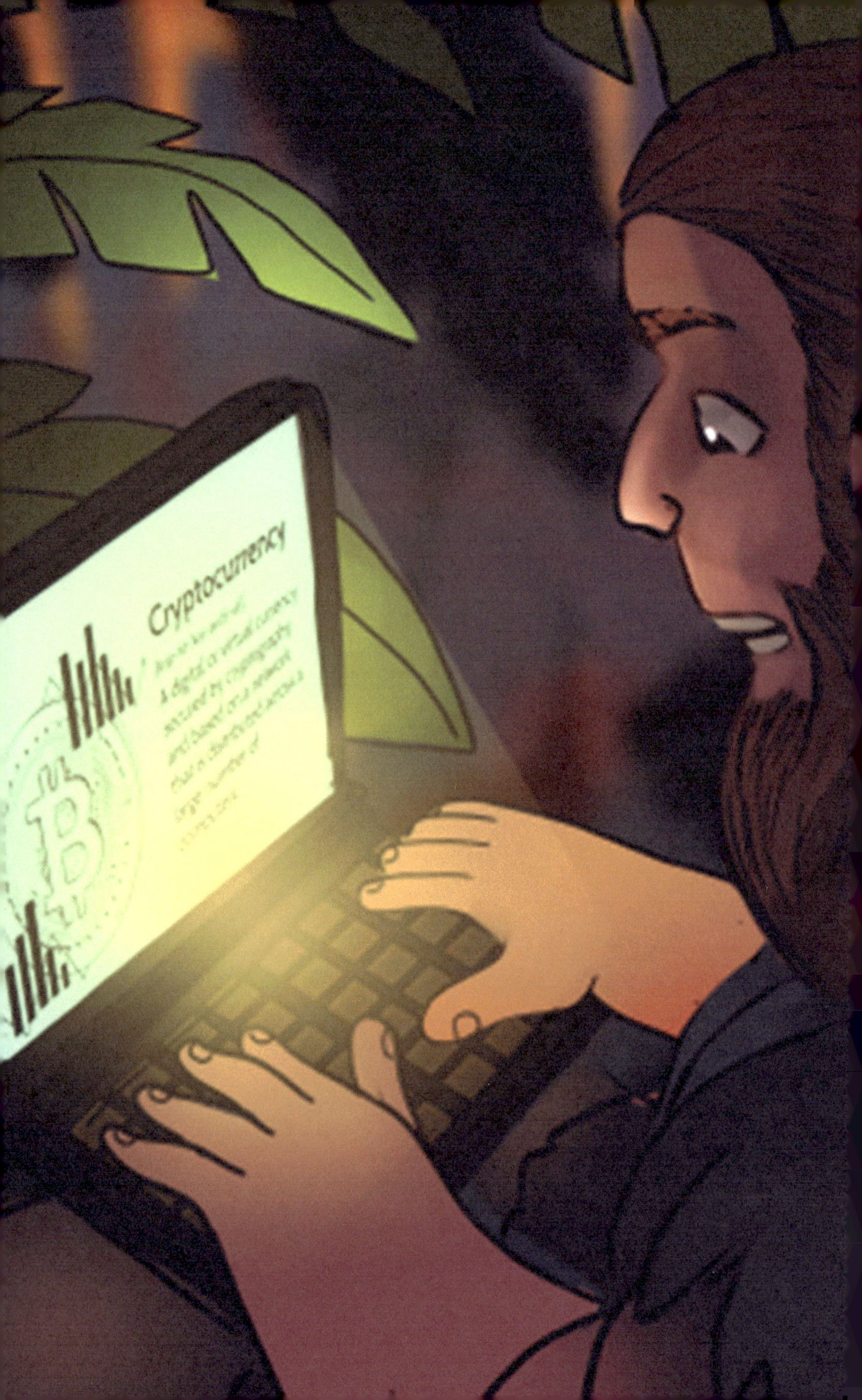
Cryptocurrency

As the Troll looked up, he felt a hard thump, the horns of Billy rammed into his hump. "My first name is Billy, and my last name is Goat; I protect new users and show them the ropes. A crypto community, stronger than you, helping and giving, is what we do."

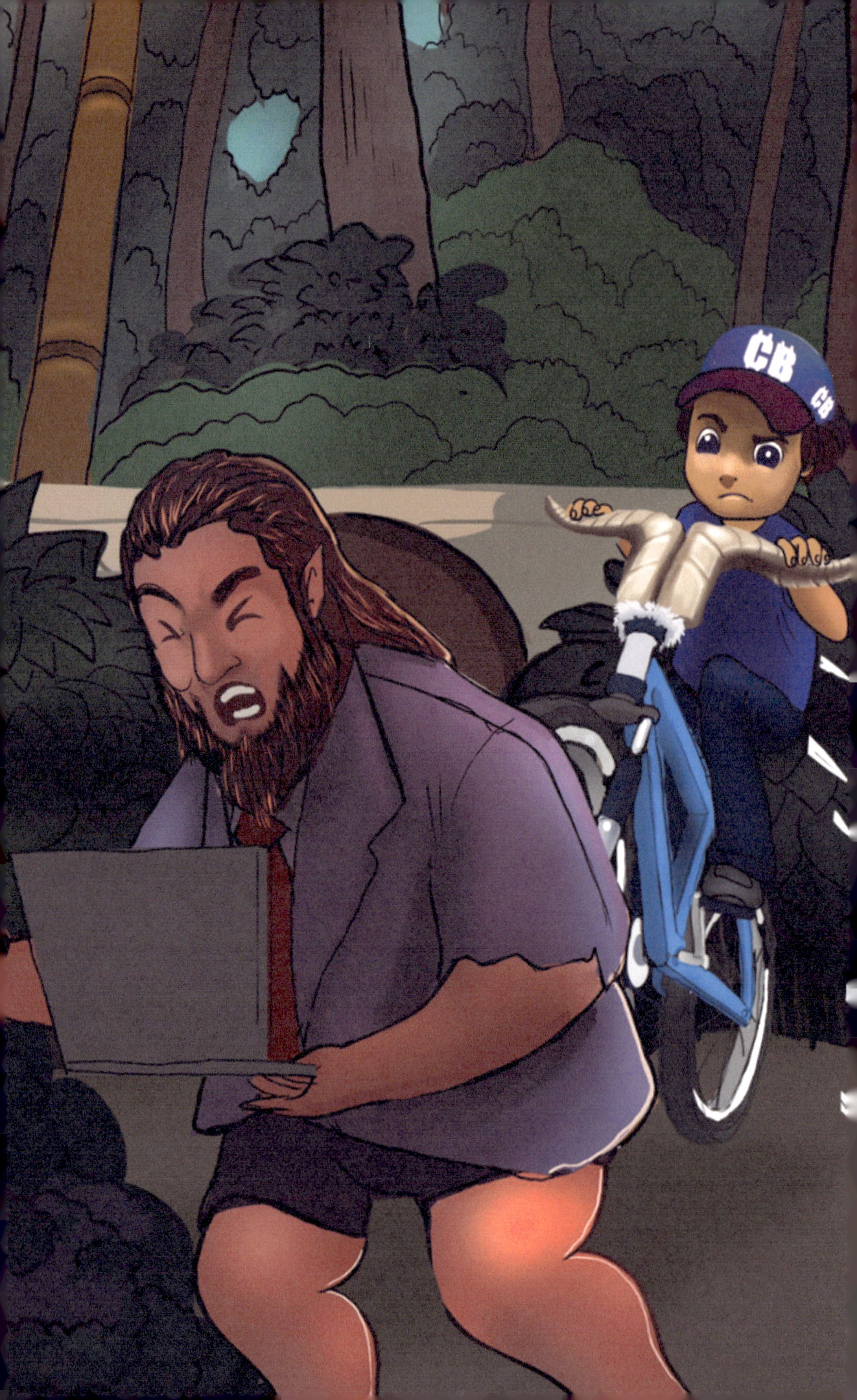
CB
CB

As the Troll looked up, he knew he had been beaten; he unplugged his computer and admitted defeat.

Billy rammed him hard and deleted his link; he told many others about Scammer Delete.

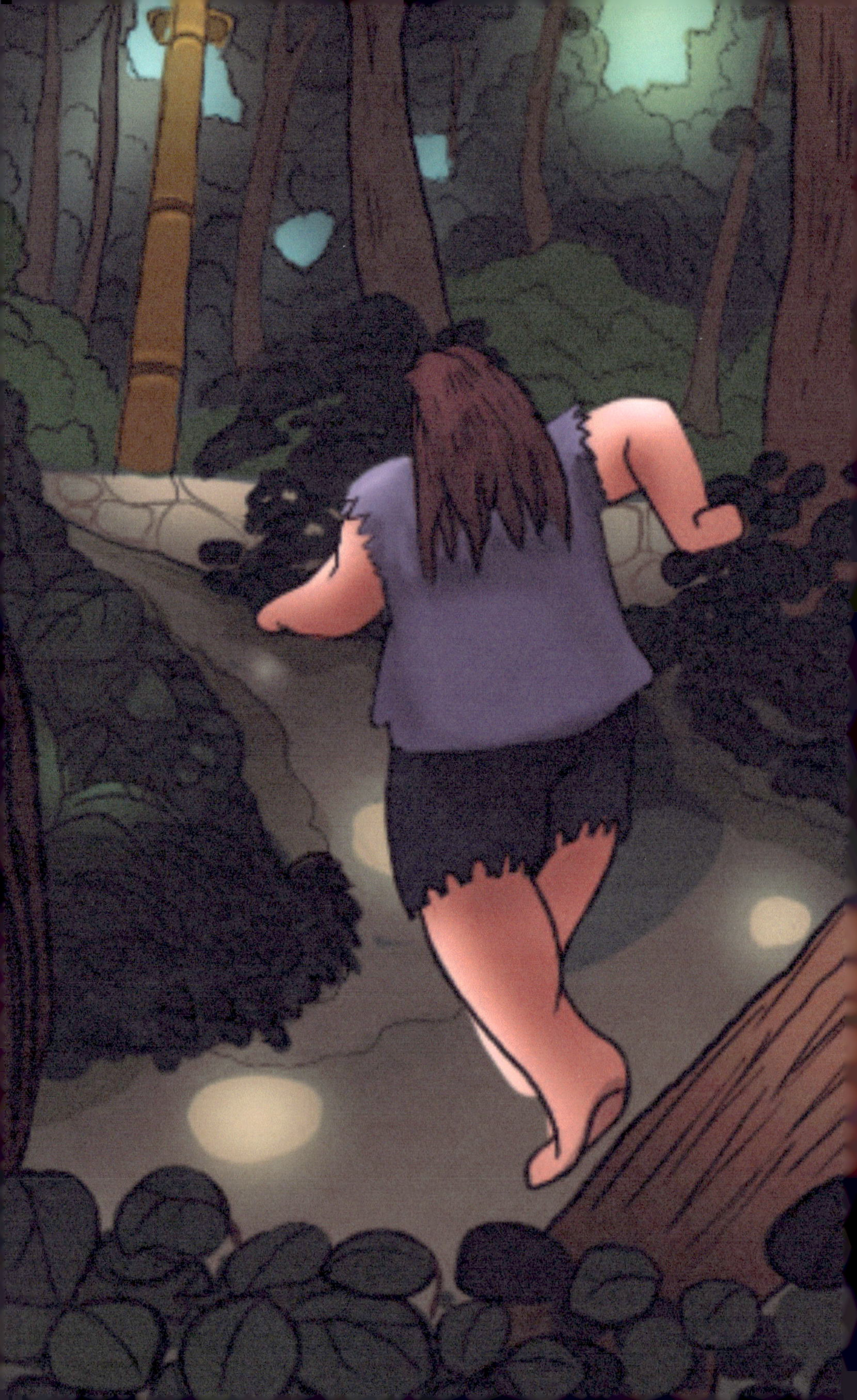

The fall off the bridge was a long way down,
a bottomless pit that could never be found.

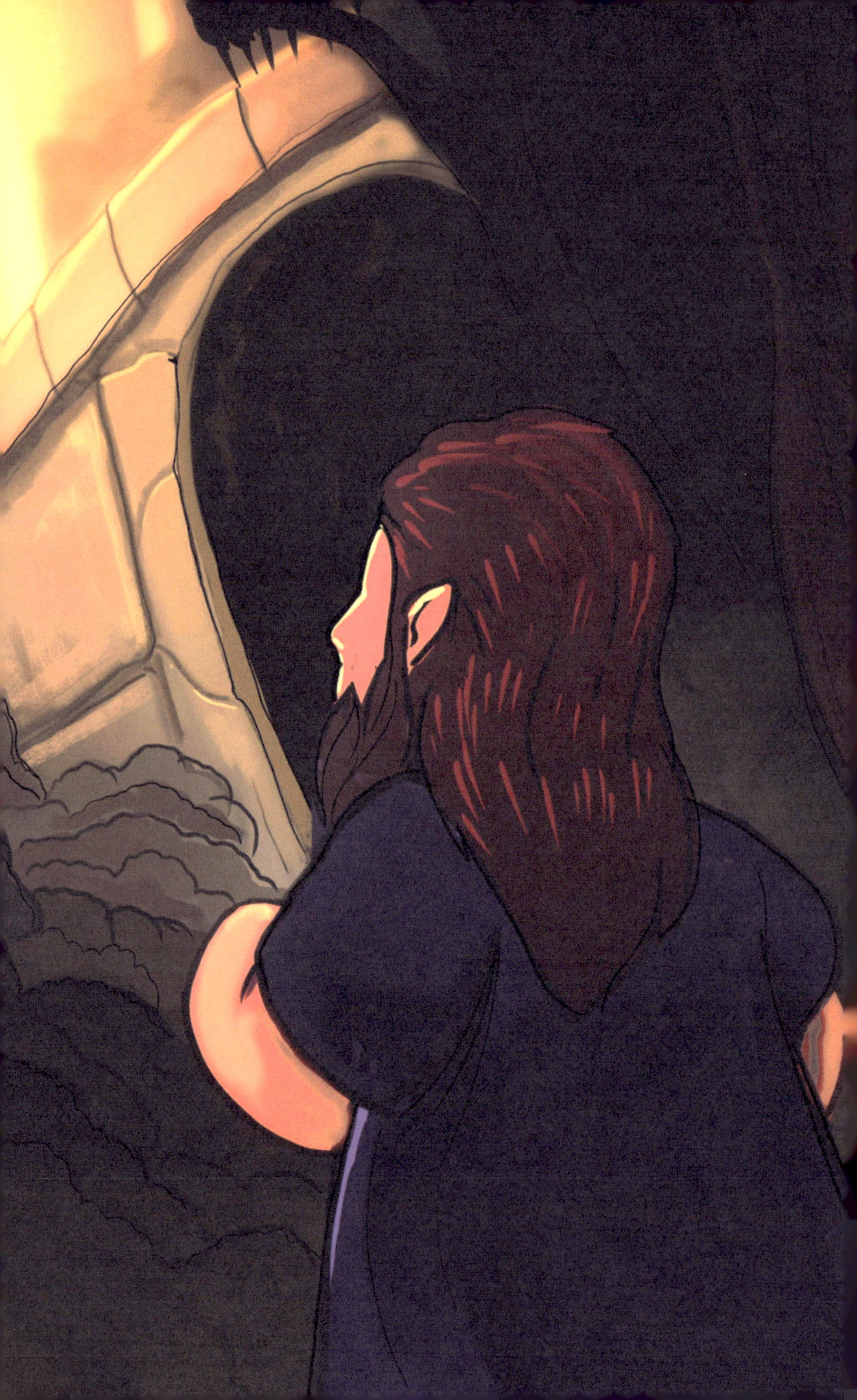

As Billy walked across the bridge, he slowly turned around and saw 10,000 users, lost and confounded. He yelled to them, "My first name is Billy, and my last name is Goat; I protect new users and show them the ropes. Listen closely, be careful, and never trust a link, or you will undoubtedly find Mr Scammer-Delete!"

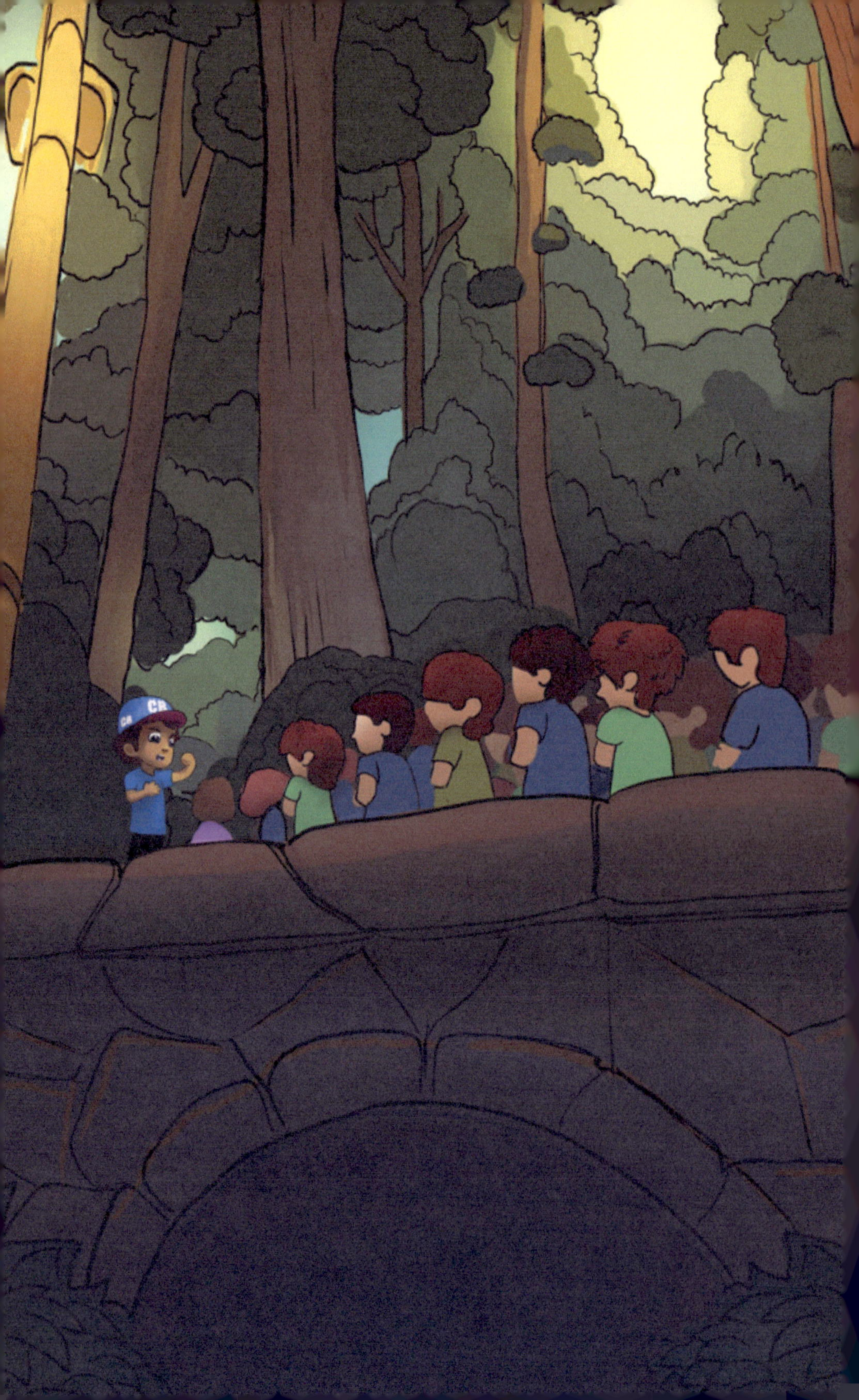

One by one, the users safely crossed the blockchain bridge and found the opportunity they sought: Bitcoin!

THE END

Made in the USA
Columbia, SC
23 October 2024